NEVER ON SATURDAY

Leaving her native France and arriving in North Wales as a postgraduate student of History and Folklore, Mel is cautiously optimistic that she can escape from her troubled past and begin a new and happier life. Then she meets Ray: charming, down-to-earth, and devastatingly handsome. Despite her failure with previous relationships, she allows herself to hope that this time, at last, she can make it work. But Mel is hiding a dark and terrible secret, which Ray must never discover . . .

SUE BARNARD

◆

NEVER
ON
SATURDAY

Complete and Unabridged

LINFORD
Leicester

First published in Great Britain in 2017
This revised edition published 2020

First Linford Edition
published 2023

A catalogue record for this book is available
from the British Library.

ISBN 978–1–4448–5000–0

Published by
Ulverscroft Limited
Anstey, Leicestershire

Printed and bound in Great Britain by
TJ Books Ltd., Padstow, Cornwall

This book is printed on acid-free paper

For R. Love always.

'What's in a name? That which we call a rose
By any other word would smell as sweet . . .'

Romeo & Juliet, Act 2, Scene 2

Acknowledgements

I remain eternally grateful to Laurence and Stephanie Patterson, of Crooked Cat Books, for believing in this story and first taking it to publication in 2017. This revised edition, reissued in 2020 in association with Ocelot Press, also owes much to their continued help and support.

I am also indebted to the following friends and writing buddies who gave much-needed encouragement and vital feedback: Ailsa Abraham, Pauline Barnett, Susan Brownrigg, Miriam Drori, Jayne Fallows, Jo Fenton, Louise Jones, Karen Moore, Lorrie Porter, Sally Quilford, Gail Richards, Helen Sea, Grant Silk and Kay Sluterbeck. Thank you, all of you. The book would be so much less without your input.

Special thanks are due to Geoff & Christine Mapp, who first introduced me to the original French legend on which the story is based.

The Palace of Curiosities, which features in Chapter Eleven, is a real and fascinating attraction. I am deeply grateful to its proprietor, the lovely David Oxley, for all his help and advice in writing the chapter about the Palace and for agreeing to let it appear in the story. For more information about the Palace, please take a look at its website: http://www.palaceofcuriosities.com.

Thanks too to everyone who left such lovely reviews for *Never on Saturday* when it was first published.

Most important of all, I could not go on writing without the unfailing support of my wonderful husband Bob and sons Nick and Chris, all of whom not only continue to indulge my whims and craziness, but actively encourage them.

Sue Barnard
December 2020

Prologue

'Daughters, for what you have done, I shall never forgive you.'

My sisters and I quailed before our mother, terrified beyond measure. Never in our lives had we witnessed such anger.

'Mother, we thought only for the best . . .'

'SILENCE! Revenge is not yours to take. But it is mine to give.'

'Revenge?'

'Ay!' She raised her hands and directed them towards my two sisters. Light flashed from her fingertips as she intoned: 'For your unnatural action, your punishment is that you shall wander the face of the earth for seven years. If during that time you encounter any human — male or female, adult or child — you shall vanish for ever.'

We stared at our mother, dumbfounded. Then she turned to me.

'But as for you,' she thundered, raising her hands again, 'since the plan for this evil deed was of your devising, your punishment shall be far greater.'

1

The air in the room was shattered by a blinding blue-green light and a deafening thunderous crash. I slammed my hands over my ears in a vain attempt to block out the sound. Through the rushing, screeching wind, I heard my mother's disembodied voice wailing:

'For what you have done, you are forever cursed. On every seventh day, you shall . . .'

The remainder of her words were lost as I drifted into blessed unconsciousness. Only later did I learn from my sisters what the dreadful nature of my punishment was to be . . .

1

Friday

'Next, please!'

Mel stepped up to the counter.

'Coffee, please.'

'What sort?' The woman behind the counter gestured towards the huge blackboard mounted on the wall behind her.

Mel frowned. In her native village in France, if you asked for '*un café*' you knew exactly what you were getting: a tiny cup, half-full or two-thirds-full of industrial-strength mud, accompanied by a sachet of sugar or a wrapped sugar-lump, and sometimes served with a small biscuit. She peered at the daunting list on the board, and her eyes widened in bewilderment. What on earth was a Macchiato? Or a Chai Latte? Or a Flat White? Or (in Heaven's name) a Hot Dutch?

'Er — just something simple, please.'

'Americano, then?'

'What's that?'

'It's a single shot of espresso in a mug of hot water.'

'Er — yes, thanks. That sounds fine.' Mel hoped she sounded more convinced than she felt. But her ordeal was by no means over yet.

'Regular, Grande or Maxima?' the woman intoned.

'What?'

'What size do you want?'

'Um. How big are they?'

The woman pointed to three different-sized mugs which were lined up along the front of the counter. The largest one, which Mel deduced must be the Maxima, was more than twice the size of the smallest one. Glancing up again at the blackboard, she was amazed to see that it was only 30p more expensive than the Grande (which, in spite of its name, appeared in fact to be medium rather than large), and only 50p more expensive than the Regular.

'That one, please.' She pointed to the

largest cup.

'Maxima, then?'

Mel nodded. *Why on earth*, she wondered privately, *can't they just call them Small, Medium and Large?*

'Milk?'

'Yes, please.'

'Ordinary or soya?'

'Er — ordinary, please.'

'Whole or skinny?'

'I'm sorry?'

The woman behind the counter took a deep breath, evidently trying to suppress a sigh of frustration.

'Would you like full-cream milk or skimmed milk?' she asked, slowly and deliberately, as if addressing a small child.

'Oh, sorry. Skimmed, please. It's just that I've never heard it referred to as 'skinny' before.'

They might just as well be talking in a foreign language, Mel thought.

'Drink here, or take out?'

'Here, please.'

'Anything to eat with it?'

'No, thank you.'

'Right.' She called over her shoulder, 'One Maxima skinny Americano to drink in,' then turned back to Mel. 'That's three pounds forty-five, please.'

Mel ferreted around in her purse and finally extracted a crumpled five-pound note. The woman handed over her change and a receipt, then pointed to a space at the far end of the counter.

'Your coffee will be ready over there.'

'Thank you.'

Mel moved on as the woman turned her attention to the next customer, who began speaking in a language which Mel didn't recognise but which she presumed must be Welsh. The woman behind the counter answered in the same tongue. This was North Wales, after all — and even in the very short while that Mel had been living here, she had heard this seemingly effortless switch between the two languages surprisingly often. Welsh was everywhere. Even all the signs appeared to be bilingual, and, on that basis, Mel had managed to work out what a few of the words must mean. Of these words, the most important, so far, was *Merched* — although that carried another clue in the form of the standard international logo on the outside of the toilet door. But Welsh certainly looked as though it would be a difficult language to master, as the words seemed to be almost entirely devoid of vowels. Even the woman who had taken her order was, according to her name badge, called Myfanwy. Mel had absolutely no idea how that was supposed to be pronounced. My Fan . . . ?

No. Let's not even go there. Crikey, I thought my own name was tricky enough.

'One Maxima skinny Americano to drink in?'

'Here, please.' Mel held up her hand.

'Here you are. Sugar's on the table over there. Enjoy!'

The speaker was a tall, dark-haired man wearing a black barista apron. Mel guessed that he was probably in his mid to late twenties. She smiled her thanks, carefully picked up the huge brimming mug, and made her way to the only vacant table, which was still strewn with the detritus left by its previous occupants.

'Hang on a minute,' the barista called over from the counter. 'I'll come and clear that for you.'

'Thanks,' Mel answered, as she fished a pen and paper out of her bag.

'Sorry about this,' he said, as he leaned over the table and began to load the dirty mugs, plates, cutlery and crumpled serviettes on to a tray. 'We've been run off our feet this afternoon. It's always like this on Fridays — I think the world and his wife must reckon they've earned it by this time of the week. There you go!' He gave the table a deft wipe, quickly disposing of the remaining crumbs.

'Thank you.' Mel looked up at him and smiled. She noticed that he was wearing a badge which told the café's customers that his name was Ray. *At least that's easy to pronounce*, she found herself thinking. Not like poor *Mywhatshername over there* . . .

He smiled back. His eyes were the colour of plain chocolate. His voice also made her think of chocolate: rich, smooth and sensual.

Stop it, she told herself firmly, as she forced herself to turn her attention back to writing out her shopping list. *In any case, he must think I'm a total airhead. Especially, if he overheard me trying to order the coffee. I must have sounded really dense.*

She lifted up the mug and took a cautious sip. The hot liquid wasn't unpleasant, so long as she didn't think of it as coffee.

★ ★ ★

Mel drained the last of her coffee and made her way out into the street. She'd noticed earlier that there was a small supermarket just around the corner from the café. Knowing that she would have no chance to go shopping the following day, she recognised that here was a good opportunity to buy what she would

9

need for the weekend. She soon discovered that the supermarket didn't carry an enormous range of foodstuffs, and it didn't have everything that she wanted, but by making a few judicious substitutions she calculated that she definitely wouldn't starve.

What she hadn't anticipated was that the single shopping bag she had brought with her wasn't big enough to hold everything she bought. Reluctantly, she asked for a carrier bag, despite knowing that it would add an extra 5p to her bill, but relaxed slightly when the kindly-looking cashier gestured towards a boat-shaped box next to the till.

'We have to charge for the bags,' the cashier explained, 'but it's up to us what we do with the money, so we prefer to give it to the lifeboats.'

Mel smiled as she took the bag. 'That's a very good cause.'

It doesn't look very strong, she thought, as she began to pack her shopping away. She put the heavier items in her shopping bag, leaving the flimsy carrier bag for a packet of breakfast cereal, a box of tissues, a bottle of shampoo and a loaf of bread. Bidding a cheerful goodbye to the friendly cashier, she heaved her handbag on to her shoulder, picked up the bags and began to make her way back along the high street.

The carrier bag, although not heavy, proved to be an awkward shape, and very uncomfortable to hold. The corners of the cereal packet stuck defiantly through the thin layer of plastic, and dug painfully into Mel's calf as she struggled along. As she stopped to change hands, one of the sharp corners pierced the plastic completely. It was only a matter of a few seconds before the bag split along its entire length, depositing its contents in an untidy heap on the pavement.

'*Merde!*' Mel spat, as she bent down to retrieve them.

'I beg your pardon?'

Mel glanced up at the sound of the voice — and found herself gazing into the lovely chocolate-brown eyes of the friendly barista. Her carrier bag had given up the ghost right outside the café.

'Sorry,' she muttered. 'I didn't mean to swear out loud.'

'Oh, hello again! Herc — let me help you with those.'

Mel smiled gratefully. 'That's very kind of you. I won't turn down an offer like that! But I wouldn't want to keep you from your work.'

'You aren't. I've just finished for the afternoon.' Her new companion returned the smile, and Mel felt her knees go weak.

'What happened?' he asked, as he picked up the boxes and arranged them into a neat pile.

'I ended up buying more stuff than would fit in my shopping bag, and I had to buy an extra carrier bag.' She sighed. 'It's my own fault, I suppose, trying to get away with only buying one. I should have realised it wouldn't be enough.'

He tucked the pile of boxes under his arm, straightened up, and offered Mel his free hand to help her to her feet. His hand felt warm, strong, and strangely comforting.

'Where are you parked?'

'I'm not. I walked here.'

'Really?' He seemed surprised. 'Where from?'

'I live about ten minutes from here. I've got a room in one of the student houses, just on the other side of the main road.'

'Are you at the university?'

'Well, sort of. I'm doing — *comment dit-on?* — post-graduate studies.'

'Well, let me give you a lift. My car's just around the corner. Or, at least,' he grinned, 'I hope it is. That's where I left it this morning. There's no point in lugging this lot further than you have to.'

Mel opened her mouth to protest, but what came out was, 'Thank you. That would be lovely.' She fell into step beside him as they threaded their way along the crowded pedestrianised street.

'Here we are!'

He stopped alongside a red hatchback, parked in the shade of a high wall which ran alongside the pavement. After opening the boot and stowing Mel's shopping

13

inside, he turned to her and extended his hand.

'Perhaps we should introduce ourselves. I'm Ray Wynn Jones.'

Mel took the proffered hand. 'Lovely to meet you properly, Ray. I'm Mel de Lusignan.'

'De Lusignan? That's an unusual name.'

'It's French.'

'Really? Are you French? I must confess I was fascinated by your accent. But you speak really good English, if you don't mind my saying so.'

Mel blushed. 'Thank you. I'm not managing terribly well with Welsh, though.'

'I don't think that will be a problem. I know Welsh is spoken quite a bit round here, but everyone speaks English too.'

Mel smiled. 'That's a relief!'

'And Mel? What's that short for? Do I call you Melanie? Or is it Melissa?'

She shook her head, reluctantly withdrew her hand, and gave a guarded smile.

14

'I prefer just Mel.' *That's all you need to know.*

Just stick to the basic facts, she told herself. *Don't elaborate. You might have already given too much away . . .*

★ ★ ★

'You are the fairest maiden that I have ever beheld.'

I lowered my head and stared into the depths of the water. Although I felt complimented by his words, I was nonetheless embarrassed by his attention. We were alone by the fountain in the forest of Colombiers, with only a pale moon to relieve the darkness around us. My two sisters, who had been my companions thus far, were now nowhere to be seen.

'You flatter me, kind sir.'

''Tis not flattery, 'tis but the truth. Never in my life have I seen such beauty. Please, fair lady, do not avert your eyes. Look upon me.'

I raised my face and met his gaze. His countenance was kind and gentle, though I

15

discerned a troubled look in his dark eyes.

'Pray, kind sir, please tell me how you came to be here?'

His face grew grave.

'Lady, I am afeared to tell you.'

'Please, sir, do not be. I will listen to your tale.'

He breathed in deeply, as if mustering the courage to continue, then began to recount the story of his recent misadventure.

'I was hunting with my master in the forest . . .'

'Your master, sir?'

'Forgive me, lady. I refer to the Lord Emmerick, the most noble Count of Poitou.'

'Indeed?' Although I had never previously encountered the Lord Emmerick, I had often heard my parents speak of him. He was a nobleman of great wealth, and withal a kindly and a virtuous man. This fellow now standing before me was fortunate to be in the employ of such a lord as he.

'Indeed. We were hunting a wild boar, here in the forest. My master and I followed the beast at great speed into the depths of the woods, but it outran us, and we then

16

discovered that we had become separated from our retinue. By now night had fallen, and we knew that we should not attempt to find our way back to the castle until daylight. We therefore gathered together such dry wood as we could find, and with our combined efforts we succeeded in lighting a fire. We were warming ourselves by the flames, when we heard a most terrible noise in the trees behind us.'

He paused. It fell to me to break the silence.

'Pray, good sir, do continue.'

He drew another deep breath.

'We turned, and beheld the boar which we had been hunting for the entire day. It was bearing down upon us at great speed, and I feared for my good master's life.'

'Did you not fear for your own life, sir?'

'Nay, fair lady, not for a moment. I already owed my life to my master. I held his life in much higher esteem than my own.'

I opened my mouth to answer, then it came to me that he had spoken of his master's life in the past tense, not the present.

'Why, good sir, do you say 'held' rather than 'hold'?'

17

He shuddered.

'*I drew my sword and made to attack the beast. I felt the blade hit home, but the beast did not fall. I struck again, and this time my aim was true — the beast lay dead at my feet. I withdrew my sword from the beast's side and turned to my master — and it was then that I perceived that my first strike had disastrously miscarried. The blade had struck my beloved master. He was most cruelly and tragically slain. And by my own hand.*'

2

Friday

'This is really most kind of you, Ray.' Mel smiled gratefully as she finished putting the perishables into the fridge. 'Can I offer you some coffee?'

Ray grinned as he sat down at the table in the communal kitchen. 'I'd prefer tea, if you don't mind.'

Mel's smile faded. 'I'm afraid I'm not very good at making tea. We don't drink it very often in France.'

'In that case,' Ray beamed, 'I shall have to teach you. Do you have any proper teabags?'

Mel frowned. 'Not of my own. But there might be some in the cupboard. If we use those, I can buy a new pack next time I go shopping.'

Ray hunted through the cupboards and eventually extracted a battered packet.

'Hmm. Own-brand, but these will

have to do. Where's the teapot?'

'Over there by the sink.'

Ray picked up the pot, removed the lid, and winced. 'When was this last used?'

Mel shrugged. 'I've no idea. Why do you ask?'

By way of answer, Ray held out the pot and Mel peered inside. Her nostrils were attacked by a sharp but musty stench, and in the murky depths of the pot she could just make out the shapes of two mouldy teabags, floating miserably on the surface of a dark brown scummy liquid.

'*Mon Dieu!*' Mel muttered under her breath.

'Quite,' Ray agreed. 'This is going to need a thorough clean before we can use it. Could you boil some water, please?' He smiled sheepishly. 'And to think I thought I'd finished making hot drinks for today!'

'Sorry!' Mel returned the smile as she filled the kettle. 'Was it that bad?'

Ray grinned. 'Well, no. Just frantically

busy. But then, Fridays always are. And my feet are killing me.'

Mel chuckled. 'It seems odd to hear a guy say that. It's usually girls who are the ones who complain. Mainly because they're wearing stupidly high heels!'

She followed Ray's gaze as it travelled downwards, eventually settling on her simple ballerina pumps.

'You're not a shoe person, then?'

Mel shook her head, silently cursing herself for having brought up a topic she wasn't happy to discuss.

'Never really seen the point of it,' she muttered, desperately trying to sound as though footwear genuinely didn't matter to her. 'Where are you off to after this?' she added hastily.

Damn. That's what comes of trying to change the subject quickly. Now he probably thinks I'm trying to get rid of him.

Fortunately, though, Ray didn't seem to have noticed anything untoward. He tipped the contents of the teapot into the sink, then retrieved the mouldy teabags and threw them into the bin.

'Nowhere special. Look, it's a nice afternoon — after we've had this tea, do you fancy coming for a walk? Have you ever been to look at the pier?'

'No. I've only been here for a few days, and I still don't really know Bangor very well at all. But I thought you said your feet were killing you!'

Ray grinned. 'Only from standing for too long. Once I've had a sit down I'll be fine. And I can always find enough energy for a stroll!'

'Wow, it's impressive, isn't it?' Mel gazed at the long, ornate Victorian structure, stretching out across the Menai Straits. From one angle, it appeared to reach almost as far as the Isle of Anglesey on the other side of the water.

Ray nodded. 'I quite often come for a walk along here. It's particularly good when the tide's out; you see all sorts of seabirds on the mudflats.'

'Are you a birdwatcher, then?'

'Not a serious one, but if I see one I like to know what it is. I learned a bit about them when I was at uni.'

'Oh, yes? Why was that?'

'I studied marine biology.'

'Oh!' Mel gasped.

'What's the matter?'

'Nothing,' Mel lied. She prayed that he hadn't noticed her alarm. 'It's just that . . .' She thought quickly. 'Well . . . I didn't expect to find a marine biologist working in a coffee shop!'

'I must be honest,' Ray sighed, 'working in a coffee shop wasn't exactly my first choice! But jobs in marine biology are pretty few and far between. And even unemployed marine biologists have to keep body and soul together somehow. But hey, that's more than enough about me. What about you?'

'What about me?' Mel asked nervously.

'What are you doing in Bangor? You're at the university, you said?'

Mel stared out across the Straits, as if admiring the view of the island, as she tried to compose an answer. She didn't want to tell an outright lie, but how much — or how little — could she get away with telling him?

'I'm studying history and folklore,' she began cautiously, without taking her eyes off the view.

'Oh yes? That sounds fascinating. Are you familiar with the Mabinogion?'

'No — what's that?'

'It's a collection of traditional Welsh tales. I studied it at school. I've got an English edition I can lend you if you're interested.'

'Thank you.' Mel turned to him and smiled with genuine enthusiasm. 'That would be lovely.'

'So, you come from France? Which part?'

'From the Vendée. It's on the west coast, just south of Brittany. There's a castle called Lusignan near the town of Vouvant. Or at least, there used to be — I think it's just a ruin now. I've always understood that it was built by one of my ancestors. I think that's where my surname comes from.' She smiled wistfully. 'I don't know how true that is, but it's a nice story.'

Ray grinned. 'I've heard people say there are some parts of Wales where you feel you could be anywhere in Brittany. Is that what's brought you here?'

Mel shook her head. 'Not entirely,' she answered quietly. 'My parents died, and I felt as though I needed a new start somewhere else.'

Ray whistled under his breath. 'I'm sorry to hear that. I . . .' His voice trailed off.

Mel got the impression that he was even less comfortable talking about this than she was. There was an awkward pause.

'But I've sort of got used to it now,' she said eventually. 'I try not to think about it too much. And I love it here. I'm very much an outdoor girl. I walk, I swim, and, yes, I like birdwatching too.'

Ray's face brightened visibly. He waved an arm across the Menai Straits towards the Isle of Anglesey. Its bright colours — the greens, reds and yellows of the landscape contrasting with the sharp blue of the sky above and the mellow green of the water below — sparkled in the late afternoon sun.

'Have you been across to the island?'

Mel shook her head. 'As I said, I've only recently arrived here.'

'Well, how do you fancy going for a birdwatching walk over there? There's a super beach down on the south coast where you can see all sorts of things.'

Mel beamed. 'Thank you, that would be lovely. When did you have in mind?'

'How about tomorrow?'

Merde, Mel thought. *Here we go again . . .*

'Sorry,' she muttered, staring at the ground. 'I can't manage tomorrow.' *Please don't ask me why not . . .*

'Well, how about Sunday, then?' Fortunately, Ray appeared to accept her answer without seeming to be too inquisitive.

She forced her face back into a smile before looking up at him. 'Sunday would be lovely. Thank you.'

★　★　★

His last words were lost in a racking sob. Notwithstanding my own shock at what he had just told me, I gently laid my hand upon his arm.

'When did this happen?' I asked.

'Not a half-hour since. Once I became aware of the foul deed I had done, I mounted my horse and fled, with no notion of which direction I was travelling. And thus it was, fair lady, that I chanced upon this fountain, and beheld you and your companions. Truth to tell, I believed that I was in the presence of angels.'

I smiled at his words. 'Believe me, good sir, I and my companions — who you can see have now both left us — are not angels. The other two ladies whom you saw are my sisters. But, by your leave, sir, may I offer you counsel? I believe I can see a way for you to escape from your sad situation.'

'How so?' he asked.

'You must remount your horse and return forthwith to the Lord Emmerick's castle. Say nothing to anyone of what has befallen you here in the forest. You have said yourself that you and your master became separated

from the rest of your hunting companions. It is my firm belief that they too will have lost themselves in the forest, and all will by now have returned to the castle by their own means. Indeed, it may well be that your companions as yet have no notion that your master has not returned. None, save you and I, know of what has truly occurred; thus, no suspicion concerning your master's misfortune can attach itself to you. When daylight comes, and the courtiers become aware that he is not among them, only then will the alarm be raised. In the fullness of time, the forest will be searched and your master's corpse will be discovered, but it will be found in such close proximity to the dead wild boar that all will conclude that both were slain, each by the other, in a tragic fight.'

The gentleman was silent for a few moments as he considered this, then he turned to me with a wondrous smile on his countenance. From his eyes shone joy and relief by turns.

'Dearest lady, you have lifted an unbearable burden from my shoulders. How can

I ever hope to repay you for your kindness and wisdom?'

'By taking heed of what I have told you, good sir, and by not placing yourself in renewed danger.'

A strange light came into his eyes at these words.

'You have a care for my safety, then?'

I was silent, and lowered my gaze so that he might not see my burning cheeks. Although I knew that this young man had indeed touched my heart, in a way in which no other suitor had ever succeeded in doing, I was ashamed for whatever forwardness I had displayed. Such conduct was, I had always been advised, deemed unbecoming for a lady of any rank.

'Ay, sir, I do,' I whispered.

'Dare I hope that you might also have a care for me?'

'Sir,' I answered, 'you barely know me.'

By way of answer, he placed his hand beneath my chin and gently raised my face, so that I might look him in the eye.

'It is true that I have only just encountered you, and yet I feel as though I have

known you for my entire life. So much so that already I find it impossible to envisage a life without you.'

'Truly, sir?'

'Truly, fair lady. And despite your modest poise and your non-committal words, I can discern in your eyes that you might also return my affection. The eyes are indeed the windows of the soul.'

His words were true. However much I might wish to conceal the level of my feelings, my eyes could hide no secrets. Yet I, who had lately been the one to counsel him, could now find no words with which to answer.

This time, it fell to him to break the silence. He took hold of my hand and knelt down on one knee before me.

'Lady, I must ask you outright: will you be my wife?'

3

Sunday

Mel awoke to a bright clear morning. She sat up in bed and massaged her calves, then went into her ensuite bathroom to refresh herself with a welcome shower before settling down to make her breakfast. Since moving into the house, her days had usually begun in the chaos of a student kitchen, during which she'd gulped down a hasty bowl of cereal and a glass of orange juice whilst trying to avoid getting in everyone else's way. But today, knowing that the other occupants of the house probably wouldn't surface much before midday, she allowed herself the luxury of something a little more special — a plate of wholemeal toast topped with scrambled eggs and smoked salmon, washed down with freshly-brewed ground coffee.

She was just finishing the washing-up when her phone rang. A spontaneous smile came to her face as she recognised Ray's name on the display — but then turned to a frown as she wondered why he should be calling her. Was he ill? Or had he had second thoughts about their planned outing?

'Ray? Are you all right?'

'Yes, everything's fine. Are you still OK for today?'

'Yes, why?'

'I've just looked at the weather forecast, and it sounds as though it's going to be a hot one. So pack some sun cream, and bring your swimsuit and a towel. There are some lovely beaches on the island, so it would be nice to be able to have a swim if we want.'

'That sounds lovely. Do you want me to bring anything else?'

'Have you got any binoculars?'

'I'm afraid not. Is that going to be a problem?'

'No, I've got a spare pair I can lend you. And I was thinking of bringing a picnic. Is that OK with you?'

'Yes, thanks. That sounds lovely.'

'Great. I'll pick you up in about half an hour. Oh — one other thing: the paths can be a bit steep and stony, so make sure you wear suitable shoes.'

Shoes? Oh no, not again . . .

'What sort of shoes?' Mel answered aloud, desperately hoping that her voice sounded normal.

'Oh, trainers or something similar. Something you'll be comfortable walking in. Just don't wear sandals.'

'All right, thanks. *À toute à l'heure.*'

She ended the call then bent down and carefully massaged her calves again. Her legs felt uncomfortably stiff. But with any luck, a decent walk would help to improve the circulation. She certainly hoped so.

★ ★ ★

'I had no idea that Anglesey would be like this,' Mel said in amazement, as Ray negotiated the car along the narrow road which wound its way through the pine forest towards the beach. The verges were peppered with small flowers the colour of fresh butter. 'It reminds me very much of the French Atlantic coast.'

'In what way?' Ray asked, amused.

'Well, there are lots of places where there are pine forests alongside the coast. There's a particularly lovely one on the Île d'Oléron.'

'Where's that, exactly? I'm afraid I don't know that area of France. Come to that, I don't really know France at all. I've been to Paris a few times, but the rest of the country is pretty much uncharted territory.'

'Do you know where La Rochelle is?'

'Vaguely. About halfway down the coast, isn't it?'

Mel nodded. 'The Île d'Oléron is a little way further south. It has beautiful beaches, and a pine forest just like this.' She paused and inhaled deeply through the open car window. 'It even smells the same,' she added with a wistful smile.

'I must admit I was never very good at geography,' Ray admitted, after a moment. 'I've heard of La Rochelle, but that was more because of history. I can't remember many of the details, but wasn't there some big massacre there, or something?'

Mel nodded. 'Not a massacre as such, but it does have a pretty violent history. There was a long siege there, during the Wars of Religion.'

'Oh, yes? What happened?'

'Have you heard of the St Bartholomew's Day massacre?'

'Yes, but I don't know very much about it.'

'It was a massacre of the Protestant Huguenots in Paris during the late sixteenth century. Some people believe that Catherine de Medici might have been behind it. I don't know whether that's true or not, but she was a very unpopular queen, so it was easy to pin the blame on her. Anyway, after the massacre, the Huguenots got the message that they weren't popular with the Catholics, so a lot of them fled to La Rochelle. It was a well-fortified city, and had access to the sea, so they thought they'd be safe there.

But all that happened was that they ended up being surrounded and starved out for months on end.' Mel shuddered.

'You seem to know a lot about this,' Ray remarked.

Mel silently cursed herself for having said so much. She hoped that he wouldn't be suspicious about the depth of her knowledge of French history.

'Not really,' she said aloud. 'It's only what's taught in schools in France. I expect you know a lot of British history that I wouldn't know anything about.'

Ray grinned. 'Well, we had all sorts of stuff rammed down our throats at school, but I'm afraid I only remember the bits I found interesting.'

'Oh, yes?' Mel clutched gratefully at the conversational lifeline. 'Which bits were those?'

'The Tudors and Stuarts, mainly. Good Queen Bess, Sir Francis Drake, William Shakespeare and all that. If I remember rightly, they would have been at about the same time as what you've just described. It was a very colourful period of history, with lots of fascinating characters. Come to think of it, we even had our own version of the Wars of Religion.'

'Really?' Mel was genuinely surprised.

'Yes. It all started when Henry the Eighth wanted a divorce from his first wife . . .'

'Ah, yes. We learned a little about him at school. He had six wives altogether, *n'est-ce pas*? I always thought that was a little — how do you say? — excessive.'

'That's right. And yes, it was. But that's how it all started. He wanted a divorce but the Pope wouldn't give him one, so he broke away from the Catholic Church and set up a new church with himself as the head. Then, later, his daughter Mary became queen and tried to reconvert England back to Catholicism. She had lots of Protestants burned at the stake . . .'

'Ugh,' Mel shuddered. 'A bit like Catherine de Medici and the Huguenots?'

'Yes, I suppose so. And she was probably just about as unpopular. The people called her Bloody Mary. Then, after she died, we got Queen Elizabeth. She was Protestant, and by all accounts she treated the Catholics pretty badly. The discord went on for years. Centuries, even. Henry the Eighth has a lot to answer for.'

'How intriguing! I never knew any of this.'

'But after that, we got all sorts of boring stuff. Such as the Corn Laws, for instance. And then the repeal of the Corn Laws. I think my brain shut down when we did those!' Ray chuckled.

Relieved at having successfully diverted his attention from a potentially dangerous topic, Mel allowed herself to join in the laughter.

'I know what you mean. And I think that's probably true of most people. You remember the interesting parts, but forget the tedious ones.'

'True,' Ray agreed. 'And it's not just with history either. As soon as I was old enough to make up my own mind, I stuck with what I was really interested in. That's how I ended up doing marine biology. Ah, here we are!'

The narrow road sloped downwards through the trees and opened out into a large car park. Over to one side, Mel could see a bank of sand dunes. Beyond them, through a gap, was the sea. Further out, in the far distance, she could make out the grey silhouette of a range of mountains. Ray steered the car round the complicated one-way layout, past several rows of empty parking bays, eventually coming to a stop in a small section tucked partly out of sight in a far corner.

'I always park here,' he explained, in answer to Mel's enquiring look. 'It's shady, so the car will stay nice and cool. Do you fancy a coffee before we start?'

'What?' Mel peered around, puzzled. 'Here?'

'Over there.' Ray pointed towards the other side of the car park, where an ice-cream van appeared to be doing a roaring trade. Next to it, a queue of people were waiting by a small open-sided caravan.

'It might look pretty unassuming, but they do very good coffee.'

'OK, then.'

As they set off across the car park, Mel secretly hoped that this time she wouldn't be faced with the same mind-scrambling selection as before — she had no wish to display her ignorance for a second time. But as they approached the caravan, her nostrils were invaded by an unfamiliar yet tantalising aroma. Ray stopped and took a deep breath.

'Mmm. Bacon baps. Do you fancy one?'

'I . . . I've never tried them.'

'Really?' Ray's eyebrows shot up in amazement.

'Really. We never had them in France.' That, at least, was true enough. What she didn't want to admit to him was that she didn't even know what they were. Last Friday's coffee incident had been embarrassing enough.

'Well, Mademoiselle from La Rochelle, it's about time you did. Prepare to be educated!'

Mel opened her mouth to protest that she wasn't actually from La Rochelle, but then thought better of it, on the basis that she might then be quizzed further about where she did actually come from. Instead, she allowed Ray to guide her to a seat at a vacant picnic table before he joined the queue of customers waiting at the caravan counter. As she waited, Mel glanced around at her surroundings. To one side stood a copse of tall conifers, at the top of which she could just make out two or three flocks of small birds. She picked up one of the pairs of binoculars Ray had left on the table, and carefully focussed on the birds. They were finch-like in size and shape, but their markings looked different from the chaffinches and greenfinches she had become used to seeing in the garden of the student house.

'Here you are!' Ray had appeared at her side, clutching two large white bread rolls, each wrapped round with a paper serviette. 'Hang on to these for a moment, would you? I need to go back for the coffees.'

Mel laid aside the binoculars before lifting up the top of one of the bread rolls and peering cautiously inside. The bread itself was feather-light, and the filling consisted of two steaming slices of dark-pink meat, each edged with a strip of crisp golden-brown fat. Her mouth watered at the bewitching aroma, but she forced herself to wait until Ray had rejoined her and placed two paper cups on the table in front of them.

'So, this is a bacon bap?' she asked, as she handed one back to him.

'It is indeed!' He pulled the paper serviette aside and took a large bite from the roll, chewed for a moment, then closed his eyes as if in rapture. On opening them again, he noticed that her roll still remained untouched.

'Come on,' he urged, 'don't let it go cold!'

Mel picked up her roll and took a cautious nibble. The flavour was quite unlike anything she had ever experienced; smoky, savoury, salty and sweet, all at the same time.

'Mmm, this is divine!' she murmured. 'I can't believe I've lived for so long without tasting this.'

Ray grinned. 'And you come from France — the spiritual home of good food?'

Mel nodded as she prepared to take another bite. 'I'd always thought it was. But I suppose this must prove that there's still room to learn more!'

They finished their rolls in companionable silence. As they sipped their coffee, Mel took up the binoculars and focussed on the tops of the pine trees.

'What are you looking at?' Ray asked.

'Those birds up there. What are they?'

Ray picked up his own binoculars and followed her gaze. 'Oh, they're crossbills. They feed on the seeds from the pine-cones. Can you see the shape of their beaks?'

'Cross-bills? Oh, yes, I see now. In France, we call them *becs-croisés*. I didn't realise you had them round here. That's probably why I didn't recognise them.'

She sighed.

'What's the matter?'

Mel forced a smile. 'The last time I saw any of them was in the pine forests in the Vendée. They reminded me a little of home.'

Feeling a tear pricking the corner of her eye, she quickly turned her head away and focussed even more intently on the birds. Why did such a seemingly trivial thing as the sight of a flock of crossbills make her so upset? But she would not cry — not here, not anywhere. She would enjoy the day. Whatever else might be troubling her, she would enjoy the day.

In fact, she had another six days before she needed to trouble herself about anything at all.

Yes, she told herself firmly. She would enjoy the day.

⋆ ⋆ ⋆

'Sir, I know nothing about you, save what you have told me concerning yourself and the Lord Emmerick. I do not even know

your name.'

He rose to his feet and bowed his head.

'Forgive me, dearest lady. Grant me but a few minutes and I will tell you all. My name is Raimondin, and I am the youngest son of the Comte de la Forêt. My father is a kinsman to the Lord Emmerick. But, unlike the Lord Emmerick, my father is a poor man, with many children whom he cannot easily support. Out of compassion for our lot, the good Lord Emmerick agreed with my father that he should adopt me into his own family. He has but two children, a son named Bertram and a daughter named Blaniferte. My cousins were both happy to accept me into their household . . .'

He paused, and his face fell.

'What is troubling you, good lord Raimondin?'

'It has just come to my mind that they may not wish me to remain there, now that my cousin Bertram is become the new Count of Poitou.'

'I am sure that he would not cast you out without any land or money,' I answered carefully.

'I know that the Lord Emmerick would not have done so, but I cannot assume the same of my cousin. I know that he was my master's rightful heir, being the first-born, but as to whether any provision had been made for me after my master's death, I know not.'

'Have you considered making a request to your cousin?'

He stared at me, a puzzled expression on his countenance. Clearly this thought had not entered his mind.

'What do you suggest?'

'I suggest nothing, for the moment, but I have an idea whereby you might acquire lands and a great palace of your own.'

His gazed at me wistfully.

'What use would a great palace be to me, if I must live there alone and unloved? I ask you again, fair lady, will you consent to be my wife?'

I looked into his eyes. 'My lord, I am greatly honoured at the compliment you have paid me. But ere I answer your question, may I first ask you one of my own?'

He nodded.

'Does it not strike you as strange,' I continued, 'that you have already asked me to be your wife, yet you know nothing at all about me? Once you know the truth about me, you may wish to withdraw your proposal of marriage. Indeed, my good lord Raimondin, you do not even know my name . . .'

4

Sunday

'Shall we go?'

Mel drained the last of her coffee, wiped her mouth with the serviette, and nodded. 'Which way?'

'We've got a choice. Either along the beach, or through the forest. They're both lovely walks. If you like, we can go one way and come back the other. Which one do you want to do first?'

Mel considered. The September sun was already climbing in the sky, promising a hot and sultry afternoon.

'Beach first, I think, before it gets too hot. It might be better to leave the shady walk until later.'

'That sounds like a plan!'

Ray led the way along the sandy path which led through the gap in the dunes. Once they reached the beach, Mel noticed that the upper section, above the waterline, was covered with large pebbles which rocked and shifted under her weight.

'I'm beginning to understand why you warned me about footwear,' she gasped, as she struggled to negotiate her way across the bumpy and unstable terrain.

Ray grinned and pointed towards the sea, where the sand had been washed smooth by the outgoing tide.

'Once we're over this bit, it will be much easier, I promise you.'

I hope you're right, Mel thought. And she suddenly realised, with a lurch of the heart, that she wasn't just thinking about the pebbles.

Stop it! You've been down this road before, and it can only end in tears . . .

'Which way are we going?' she asked, once they had reached the safety of the smooth sand.

Ray gestured towards what appeared to be a large rock in the far distance.

'That way. To Llanddwyn Island.'

'An island? How will we cross to it?'

'It's only an island at high tide, and not always then. There's a sort of low causeway, and most of the time you can get to it on foot.'

'What did you say it was called?'

'Llanddwyn Island. It's the island of Saint Dwynwen. She's the Welsh patron saint of lovers.'

'Really? A bit like Saint Valentine, you mean?'

'Well, sort of. There's a ruined chapel on the island which has some connection with her. We can go and have a look at it, if you like.'

'Yes, please. It might be useful for my research.'

'OK. It might not tell you very much, but it's a nice walk anyway. And if we're lucky we might even see some seals.'

'Seals? Oh, you mean *phoques*? Do you get those here?'

'Don't sound so surprised! We might be a bit further north than what you're used to, Mademoiselle from La Rochelle, but we aren't totally uncivilised. We have our own culture, our own language, we enjoy good food, and some of us can even read!'

Mel looked up into his grinning face, and laughed gently.

'I'm sorry. I didn't mean to sound disrespectful. I was just surprised to find so many things which remind me of home.'

'Why? What were you expecting?'

'I'm not quite sure. I don't think I really gave it much thought before I left France.' She stared into space for a moment, then turned back to Ray and forced her face into a determined smile. 'I can see that there will be a lot for me to discover here. Please, show me your country!'

* * *

After I had told the lord Raimondin my name, I also told him the truth about myself: that I was a water-fae, that I had great wealth of my own, and that I possessed great magical powers. I told him also that even if he no longer wished for me to become his wife, I would nonetheless erect for him a magnificent palace on the land he would acquire from his cousin.

51

'My lady,' he said, 'from the very first moment when I set eyes upon you, I knew that there was something wonderful about you. Not merely your beauty and charm, but also something magical. In truth, I might even venture to say that you have cast a spell over me.'

I shook my head.

'Believe me, my lord, I have never used my magic to further my own ends. Such powers as I possess may only be used for the good of others.'

Once again, he knelt down upon one knee and took my hand, imprisoning it in both of his own.

'My lady, I ask you afresh: will you consent to be my wife?'

I hesitated. I wished, more than anything in the world, to be able to answer yes. Although I had known him for but less than an hour, already I knew that this man was the one with whom I wished to spend the remainder of my years.

Then I thought of the curse, fated to deny me love and happiness. How I yearned for a means whereby I might defy it . . .

5

Sunday

Ray heaved the rucksack on to his shoulders and the two of them set off walking along the firmer sand close to the edge of the sea.

Mel raised her binoculars and peered at the island in the distance.

'What's that at the far end? It looks like a windmill.'

Ray followed her gaze. 'No, it's actually a lighthouse. Or rather, it was, but I don't know if it's still in use.'

'Can we walk to it?'

'Yes, if you like. As I said, the island sometimes gets cut off, but we should be OK today.'

'Cut off?'

'Only when we get very high tides. That bit of land between the beach and the island sometimes gets flooded, and the island gets completely separated.'

Completely separated? I know how it feels . . .

'We could aim to get to the far end in time for lunch,' Ray went on. 'There are some nice little coves along the way. Some of them are quite sheltered, if you fancy a swim.'

Mel was unsure how the swimming aspect would work out, but she lowered the binoculars, smiled, and gave a non-committal nod. 'To use your words, that sounds like a plan!'

The walk towards the island was pleasant and leisurely, punctuated by occasional stops to examine the various shells, stones and seaweed left by the receding tide. Ray's knowledge of marine biology appeared to know no bounds.

'What's this?' Mel asked, picking up a strange cluster of white, papery, pea-sized objects. The whole structure was about the size of a large grapefruit.

'Those are whelk eggs,' Ray answered. 'Or, at least, the empty cases left after the baby whelks have hatched.'

'Whelks?' Mel struggled to pronounce the 'w'.

Ray bent down and picked up a large, curly shell. 'These. It's always said that if you hold one up to your ear you can hear the sea. This one is a bit damaged, but you can still see how they're supposed to look.'

'Ah! *Encornets!*' Mel smiled in recognition. 'And what about this?' She held up a tangled mass of seaweed. Attached to it, by means of a few wiry tendrils, was a dark brown translucent pouch, about an inch wide and just over four inches long.

'That's the remains of a dogfish egg. It's commonly known as a mermaid's purse. What do you call it in French?'

'I don't know.' Mel carefully bent down and returned the seaweed and its curious appendage to the sand. 'I haven't seen one before.'

At least I'm telling the truth about that, she reassured herself.

'You certainly know a lot about sea life,' she ventured, straightening up and turning to face him.

Ray smiled. 'As I think I've told you, I studied marine biology at university.'

'Ah yes, I remember now. How long ago was that?'

'Too long ago. So long ago that I'm in danger of forgetting it all. That's one reason why I like to do these beach walks. I need to keep refreshing my memory!' His face broke into a broad grin. 'But I don't usually have such delightful company.'

Mel blushed and looked down. 'It's very kind of you to say so.'

'Just the truth.'

Something in his voice made Mel catch her breath. She looked up to find him smiling at her, but with a curious warmth in his dark eyes. He held out his hand. Her own reached out, as if of its own accord, and took it.

* * *

I opened my mouth to answer his question in the negative, but the words which emerged from my lips, as if of their own accord, were, 'I will, my lord. But subject to one condition.'

'Name it, my lady. I will grant whatever you request.'

'I must ask that I may spend each week's seventh day, the day before the holy Sabbath, in complete seclusion. Neither you, nor any other member of our household, must ever venture to intrude upon my isolation.'

He looked at me in surprise and consternation.

'It is a strange request indeed, my lady. But if by agreeing to comply with it I am thus able to claim you as my own, then I am happy to concur.'

'Thank you, my good lord. And it gives me great honour and pleasure to be able to address you thus.'

'I too, my dearest lady. And already I am counting the hours until the day of our marriage.'

6

Sunday

'What's this?' Mel asked, as they approached what appeared to be the ruins of a small stone building in the middle of a wide grassy plateau.

'This is Saint Dwynwen's chapel. Shall we stop here to have lunch?'

'That would be lovely, thank you. I'm beginning to feel quite hungry.'

'Me too. It seems a very long time since that bacon sandwich.'

Ray led the way to one of the sunny corners of the interior, opened his rucksack and pulled out a large towel, which he spread out on the ground. Mel sat down and massaged her calves, gratefully leaning her back against the sun-warmed stone wall.

'Who was Saint Dwynwen? You mentioned her before, I think, but please tell me more.'

Ray pointed in the direction of the

entrance. 'I think there's an information board over there. It probably explains her story much better than I could. Go and have a look whilst I sort out the food.'

Mel eased herself to her feet and made her way to the chapel entrance. There, as Ray had said, was a large placard. She found herself looking at an image of a young woman wearing a green dress and gold jewellery. Like Mel herself, the girl had long brown hair and striking dark eyes.

Alongside the picture, text in Welsh and English told Dwynwen's sad story. Mel read that the saint had originally been a fifth-century Welsh princess, the daughter of King Brychan Brycheiniog. Although already betrothed, Dwynwen had fallen in love with a prince named Maelon Dafodrill. When Maelon discovered that Dwynwen was to be married to someone else, he was furious and attacked her. For this, he was turned into a block of ice.

The broken-hearted Dwynwen had run away to the forest and prayed. She was visited by an angel, who granted her three wishes. Her first was that Maelon should be revived; second, that she should be able to help people who were unhappy in love; and third, that she should never again wish to be married.

Poor girl, Mel thought. *It's a pretty far-fetched story, but in some ways, I know exactly how she feels. It's rotten knowing that all your relationships are doomed to failure.*

She read on. In thanks for having her wishes granted, Dwynwen had become a nun and had come to live on the island. According to legend, she had a magical well, populated by enchanted eels which could tell the fortunes of lovesick visitors.

Mel looked again at the first part of the story, and wondered why Maelon should have 'attacked' Dwynwen when he learned that she couldn't marry him. She shuddered as she realised that the word was probably a euphemism for an 'attack' of an extremely personal nature. If that was true, then it would certainly explain why Dwynwen had wanted nothing more to do with men.

Alongside Dwynwen's picture was a drawing of how the chapel itself might have looked before it was ruined. Mel read that it had once been one of Anglesey's wealthiest churches, but that Henry VIII's split with the Catholic Church put an end to the pilgrimages which had been its main source of income. The lead and timber were subsequently removed from the roof, and the walls were left to fall down.

'It seems that your Henry the Eighth is responsible for this, too,' Mel observed as she rejoined Ray.

'Really?'

'Yes.' Mel repeated what she had read on the placard. 'But it's odd about St Dwynwen. It does seem a bit strange that someone who sacrificed her own chance at happiness should have become the patron saint of lovers.'

Ray considered. 'I never really thought of it in those terms, but yes, you're right.'

He gestured towards the food boxes

which he had arranged in the centre of the towel. 'Would you prefer cheese or tuna?'

Mel's mouth watered as she sat down. 'Could I have one of each?'

'Of course. And there's some salad in that tub.'

'Mmm. Oh — I'm sorry. I never said please. It all looks so appetising that I quite forgot my manners!'

Ray grinned. 'No matter. Here, help yourself. Cheese in that box, tuna in this one. I did two sorts in case you didn't like one. I wondered if maybe you might be vegetarian or something. We get a lot of those in the café.'

'No, I'm quite happy with fish, thank you.' Mel smiled. 'But since you've gone to all this trouble, it would be churlish of me not to have at least a taste of everything!' She picked up a sandwich from the box closer to her, and took a cautious bite.

'This is cheese?' she asked in surprise, when her mouth was empty.

'Yes. Why? What's wrong with it?'

'Nothing — it's just that it tastes — well, different.'

'In what way?'

'The flavour. It's so strong. And it feels so . . . creamy.'

'It's finest Welsh Cheddar. Don't tell me you've never had Cheddar before?'

Mel shook her head. 'We have dozens of different cheeses in France, but none of them are quite like this. They're usually much softer, and the flavour is much milder.'

'Don't you like it, then? I'm happy to eat it if you'd prefer the tuna.' Ray held out his hand as if to take the sandwich from her, but she grinned and shook her head again.

'*Au contraire!* It's delicious. It's just that the taste came as a surprise. First the bacon, now this! How many other treats does this country have in store for me?'

'Wait and see,' Ray answered with a wink. 'But in the meantime, I'd better grab one of the cheese sandwiches whilst there are still some left. I can see that if

I'm not careful, you'll end up eating the lot!'

* * *

We lingered by the fountain in the forest until the first rays of the morning sun began to illuminate the sky through the canopy of leaves above our heads.

'It is time for you to return to the castle, my lord,' I told him.

He gazed at me with sadness in his eyes. 'I do not wish to leave you, my lady.'

I smiled into his eyes. 'It will only be for a short while, my lord. I will remain here and await your return. But you must take heed of what I told you concerning the Lord Emmerick. If you still wish that no suspicion should attach to you in the matter of his death, then you must play your part as I have advised you.'

He nodded and gave a wistful smile. 'Ay, my lady, you are right. I will return to the castle and will join the search party.'

He rose from where we were seated and prepared to mount his horse.

'*What of my cousin?*' he asked.

'*Say nothing to him until after the Lord Emmerick's corpse has been discovered, and all are agreed upon the manner of his demise. Then, I will advise you of what you must ask.*'

7

Sunday

'Time for a swim, then?'

They had now settled themselves in a small sandy cove towards the far end of the island. Ray got to his feet, then paused and picked up his binoculars.

'What are you looking at?'

'Over there — just to the left of that big rock. A seal!'

'OOH!' Mel grabbed her own binoculars and followed his gaze to where a small grey head was poking above the water. The two of them watched until it disappeared under the waves, at which point Ray put his binoculars down.

'We won't see him again for a while. They can stay underwater for ages, and even when he comes up again it might be a long way away. Come on, let's go.' He squared his shoulders strode purposefully across the sand towards the sea.

'Just a minute!'

Mel tucked her clothes neatly into her beach bag and adjusted the straps of her swimsuit. By the time she was standing up, Ray had already covered half the distance between them and the edge of the water. As she watched him, her eyes took in every detail — his tall, lithe body, his suntanned skin glistening with sun cream, and the shiny waves of his dark glossy hair. She caught her breath.

Mon Dieu. He's absolutely gorgeous.

'Is it cold?' she called, seeing him wince as the water covered his ankles.

'Come and find out for yourself!' he shouted back, laughing, as he carried on pressing his way through the shallows and out towards the deeper water. 'But be careful! It shelves quite steeply here!'

Sure enough, he had by now reached a point where the sea suddenly came up to his waist.

'Here goes . . .'

He took a deep breath and lunged forward so that the water now covered his shoulders. He splashed around and grinned.

'Come on. It's lovely once you're in!'

'Ok, I'm on my way!'

Mel put up a hand to shield her eyes from the sun as it glinted off the surface of the sea. Despite being no stranger to swimming in open water, she had no idea how this would compare with what she had been used to back in France. She braced herself as she approached the edge of the shallows, but was caught unawares by a rogue wave which hurtled across the beach and covered her feet with foam and seaweed.

'Ouch!' she yelled. 'It's freezing!'

'No, it isn't! As I said, it's lovely once you're in. And you've already got the first bit over with — that's the worst part. Come on! Or have I got to come and get you?'

Don't tempt me. If you come and get me, I've no idea what I'll . . .

'No, it's all right,' she answered aloud, beating her dangerous thoughts into submission as she started to wade towards him. 'I'll be with you in a min— Oh!'

The sea-bed suddenly fell away under

her feet, and the waves covered her head as she crashed headlong into the water. Gasping with surprise, she forced her face above the surface, pushing her hair out of her eyes as she struggled to regain her balance.

'Mel? Are you all right?'

Mel looked up through eyes which were stinging with salt water. Ray was now standing right beside her, putting out a hand to steady her. Despite the chill of the water, her pulse raced at his touch. She caught her breath again, hoping desperately that he would think her gasps were still the result of trying to get her breath back after her sudden submersion.

'Yes, thanks, I'm OK. I should have been more careful — you did warn me about it shelving. It just caught me by surprise, that's all . . .'

Her voice trailed off as she looked up into his dark, smouldering eyes. She was vaguely aware that his other hand had found its way round the back of her head and was gently drawing her face towards his own. Then his arms tightened around her, and the faint taste of salt on his lips gave way to a warm sweetness. Her lips gently parted as his tongue eased its way between them.

Oh Ray, this is everything I've always dreamed of. I can't let you go. Can I possibly find a way to make it work this time?

* * *

As the afternoon shadows began to lengthen, I heard the sound of approaching hoofbeats. I looked up, and beheld my promised lord emerging into the clearing. He swiftly dismounted from his horse and secured the beast by its reins to a nearby chestnut tree.

I walked across to him, and he greeted me with a warm embrace.

'What happened today at the castle?' I asked.

'All was as you foresaw, my lady. On returning to the castle, I learned that all those from the hunting party had safely returned, save for myself and the Lord Emmerick. A search party, led by my cousin Bertram,

was on the point of setting out to look for us. I told my cousin that, as night had fallen, the Lord Emmerick and I had become separated in the forest, and that I, fearful of losing my way even further in the dark, had chosen to rest in the forest until I could safely find my way back to the castle in the clear light of day. I said that I believed the Lord Emmerick would have done likewise, and I therefore feigned great concern upon being told that he had failed to return to the castle.'

I nodded. 'That was wisely done, my lord.'

'Accordingly, I agreed to join my cousin's party, which comprised perhaps a score or so of men. Once we reached the edge of the forest, we arranged to separate and search in pairs in order to cover a wider area more quickly. Ere we did so, it was agreed that whoever discovered any trace of the Lord Emmerick should give four long blasts of a hunting-horn. Those who heard it should respond with two blasts, then the discoverer should continue with a series of single blasts so that the others might be able to follow the sound.'

'A sensible and well-devised plan, my lord. It was at whose suggestion?'

He blushed modestly. 'My own, my lady. I believe I may be absorbing a little of your own great wisdom!'

'You flatter me, my lord. But please, continue.'

'My cousin Bertram rode with his squire, and I with mine. Truth to say I was afeared for my cousin, lest he might be the one to chance upon his father's corpse. But my fears were unfounded. Recalling the area where my lord had perished, I contrived that I and my squire should be the ones to search thither. And thus, we were the ones who made the grim discovery.'

He shuddered. I laid my hand upon his arm.

'But I was glad that this had befallen me, rather than any other member of the search party. Since I was the one who had, albeit by accident, been the cause of the Lord Emmerick's death, there was a certain sense of justice that I should be the one to find him.'

He shuddered again, and put his hand up to his eyes to shield them. When he lowered his hand again, I discerned the faint traces *of tears on his pale cheeks.*

'Yesternight, when the boar attacked us, it was already dark, and I could see little, save that my master and the boar were both slain. But today, in the full clear light of day, the full horrors of what I had done were plain to see. My dear master was lying in a great pool of his own blood, which had flowed unchecked from a wound in his side. Yet the wound itself appeared but slight. I'faith, dearest lady, I believe that had I but known this when the Lord Emmerick fell, I might have been able to staunch the wound and save his life.'

His last words were lost in a racking sob.

I reached up and laid my hands upon his shoulders.

'My good lord Raimondin, please do not continue to blame yourself for this. You know as well as I that you held the Lord Emmerick in the highest regard, and that you would never have wished him any harm or misfortune. What befell the two of you yesternight was a tragic accident, nothing more.'

He sighed as he glanced down at me. 'My lady, you display a wisdom well beyond your years. I will always value your counsel.'

'Thank you, my lord. But please, continue with your tale. When you and your squire were joined by the remainder of the search party, what happened?'

'My cousin Bertram wept openly at the sight of his father's corpse. Yet he, along with all others present, was willing to believe that the Lord Emmerick and the wild boar had each been mortally wounded in a chance encounter. Accordingly, the corpse of the Lord Emmerick was borne away back to the castle to await his requiem and burial.'

'When will that take place, my lord?'

'He will lie in state for another six and thirty hours. Then he will be laid to rest in the crypt of the castle, the day after tomorrow, at the hour of nine in the forenoon.'

'And then?'

'The next day, at the hour of noon, there will be a lavish ceremony at which my cousin Bertram will be enthroned as the next Count of Poitou.'

'Once that ceremony has taken place, and the attendant festivities are finished, you will need to request an audience with *your cousin to discuss the future of your own position.'*

He gazed intently at me. 'But what should I say to him concerning that future?'

'Look around us, my lord. This fountain where we are standing, and all the area around it, falls within the boundaries of the castle lands, does it not?'

'Ay . . .'

'And thus, it is the property of the Count of Poitou?'

'It is. But what of that?'

'You must ask your cousin to make a gift to you of as much ground around this fountain as can be covered and enclosed by the hide of a stag.'

He stared at me again, this time in undisguised bewilderment.

'The hide of a stag? But that will not even cover the area of the fountain itself, let alone any of the land around it!'

I smiled. 'Trust me, my good lord Raimondin. I know of a means whereby you will be able to acquire a considerable area of land. And upon this land I will use my means to erect a great palace . . .'

75

8

Tuesday

'Well, I'm glad that's over.' Ray hung up his barista apron and reached for his jacket.

'Why?' Mel asked, as she took his hand and they made their way out into the street. 'What happened?'

'Well, nothing specific, just one awkward sod after another today. It didn't help that Myfanwy had messed up the stock order yesterday, and at one point we ran out of soya milk, so I had to make a mad dash to the supermarket. I bought up their entire stock, which I don't think made me very popular with them!'

Mel gave his hand a comforting squeeze. 'Why do you need soya milk?'

'For vegans. We get quite a lot of vegetarians and vegans, especially amongst the students. Some do it for ethical reasons; for others, it's just because it's usually a lot cheaper.'

Mel smiled. 'You seem to cater very well here for people who don't eat meat. That doesn't happen very often in France. It's better now than it used to be, but there is still nothing like the choice on offer here.'

'So, how do people manage if they have any kind of food allergy? Another reason why we have to offer soya milk is that some people are allergic to dairy products.'

Mel didn't really know how to answer this, but was spared from the need to reply when Ray sighed and spoke again.

'To be honest, I'm getting a bit worried about Myfanwy.'

'In what way?'

'Difficult to say. She used to be so . . . well . . . efficient at everything, but lately she seems to be getting very forgetful. At first, I wondered if she was just under the weather, but it's been going on for a few weeks now, and she doesn't seem to be getting any better. And she seems to spend ages on the phone. She never used to do that.' He paused, staring into space. 'Am I right in thinking she served you when you came in last Friday?'

Mel nodded. 'I remember looking at her badge and thinking what an unusual name she had.'

'It's a fairly common name in Wales, but I'm not surprised you haven't come across it anywhere else.'

'But then, we have names in France which you would probably find strange. Jean-Marie, for example, or Marie-Pierre.'

Ray wrinkled his brow. 'My French isn't brilliant, but even I can recognise a few names. John-Mary or Mary-Peter? Sorry, but where on earth is the logic behind those?'

'I wish I knew. It's always puzzled me, too.'

'So what about your name? Melanie, is it? I didn't know that was a French name.'

Mel silently cursed. They had touched on a topic that she definitely didn't want to discuss. What made it even worse was that she only had herself to blame, as she was the one who had first mentioned it.

'I prefer just Mel,' she answered, forcing a noncommittal smile. She decided to try to steer the conversation back to safer, calmer waters. 'When you said her name just now, I was surprised at how you pronounced it,' she ventured. 'Where did the 'v' sound come from? There's no 'v' in the spelling.'

''V'? Oh, I see what you mean. That's the single letter 'f'. In Welsh, it's pronounced as a 'v'. If you want the 'f' sound, that's written as a 'double f'.'

'Really?'

'Yes. And there are other double letters too — 'ch', 'double d' and 'double l' — which count as a single separate letter in the Welsh alphabet. If you ever play Welsh Scrabble, those pairs of letters have a tile to themselves.'

'*Sans blague?*'

Ray looked puzzled. 'Sorry, but you've lost me. I can just about cope with *Mon Dieu*, but what on earth did you just say?'

'Sorry,' Mel answered with a smile. 'Or perhaps I should say: *désolée. Sans blague* means 'without lying'. But I know that sounds wrong in English. What would you say?'

'Probably something likc 'you're joking', I should think. Except that I'm not!'

'And from what I've seen of Welsh,' Mel went on, 'it looks as though it's rather lacking in vowels. I've seen some words which have no vowels at all.'

Ray grinned. 'But that's where you're wrong! In fact, Welsh has more vowels than English!'

'Really? How can that be?'

'The letters 'w' and 'y' are also vowels in Welsh. They're pronounced 'oo' and 'ee'.'

'How intriguing! In French, we have some letters which have accents over them, which sometimes change the sound of the letter. But in French Scrabble we ignore them.'

'Do you play Scrabble, then?'

'Sometimes. I'm not very good at it though, even in my own language, let alone anyone else's!'

'So, no chance of having a game

sometime, then?'

'I doubt it very much!' Mel gave Ray's hand another affectionate squeeze. 'But tell me, please — why are you worried about Myfanwy?' She took care to pronounce the name correctly.

'I don't know. I've just got a feeling that something isn't quite right. She's normally so sensible and reliable, but at the moment everything seems to be going wrong. And even the smallest thing seems to upset her.'

'What sort of thing?'

Ray considered. 'Well, yesterday a young woman came in with two small children. Myfanwy is usually very good with children, but on this occasion she snapped at them when they spilled their drinks. And, as I just mentioned, she messed up the milk order. That just isn't like her at all.'

'Is something worrying her, do you think? Have you asked her if there's anything wrong?'

'She hasn't mentioned anything, and I don't like to ask, in case it turns out

81

to be nothing.' Ray shrugged. 'But it's really none of my business, anyway.'

'But if it's affecting her work — and the running of the café — then perhaps it *is* your business.'

'Hmm. I hadn't thought of it like that.'

'How long has she worked there?'

'She was there when I started, and that was just over two years ago, but I don't know how long she'd been there before then.'

'So, who actually runs the café?'

Ray considered. 'Well, I suppose I do — though I've never really thought of it in those terms. I've always seen it as a team effort. And I don't own it. The owner is a guy called Geraint. He calls in every few days to check that everything is working OK. It's a good thing he wasn't there today, though.'

'Why don't you have a quiet word with him next time you see him?'

Ray frowned. 'What could I say?'

'Tell him what you've just told me. If he cares about his staff — and his business — he'll want to help.'

'Thanks. Perhaps I will. But that's enough of my troubles. What have you been doing all day?'

'Working on my — what do you call it? — thesis. But I'm quite glad to have a break from Medieval France for a while!'

'Oh, talking of breaks, that reminds me . . . What are you doing tomorrow?'

Mel considered. 'Nothing that can't wait for another day. Why?'

'Do you fancy another trip across to the island?'

'What? To the beach again?'

'Maybe, if the weather is still good — or we could explore some of the other places. There's a fine medieval town, if you fancy having a look at that.'

'Really?'

'Yes, it dates from the time of King Edward the First. Late thirteenth century, I think. Is that the same period as the stuff you're researching?'

'I think it might be a little later. But I'd love to see it.'

'That's a date, then. But for now, let's go and find a bite to eat! There's a new seafood restaurant just opened in town. And I've heard they do the most amazing local mussels.'

Mel's mouth watered. 'That sounds wonderful. I haven't had mussels since I left France.'

* * *

It was several days later that we met again by the fountain. On this occasion my lord Raimondin was accompanied by his cousin, Bertram, the newly-installed Count of Poitou.

'Greetings, fair lady,' he addressed me, not unkindly. 'My cousin Raimondin has informed me that you and he are soon to be married.'

I dropped a curtsey. 'That is true, my lord Count.'

'He has also made a request to me which, I must own, has left me a little perplexed. He has asked that I might make a gift to him of a quantity of land. That in itself I do not find unusual, but he has requested as much land around this fountain as can be covered

and enclosed by the hide of a stag.'

'That is also true, my lord Count. I have the stag hide here, ready for you.'

I gestured towards a large stag pelt which lay on the ground beside us. My lord Raimondin picked it up and made as if to spread it out on the ground, but I stayed his hand and turned again to face the Count.

'By your leave, my lord Count, do you have a sharp dagger?'

'I do, my lady, but for what purpose?'

'May I beg your leave to borrow it for a short while? All will become clear, I promise you.'

The Count unsheathed his dagger and cautiously held it out to me. I grasped the hilt, then knelt down on the ground.

'My lord Raimondin, the stag hide, if you please?'

My lord handed me the stag pelt and I spread it out upon the ground before me. Taking the Count's dagger, I made a series of long cuts which ran to and fro along the length of the hide, thus creating one continuous and slender thread. This thread, when I had finished my task, could be extended to *cover a goodly number of miles.*

The Count and my lord both watched me, open-mouthed. As I returned the dagger to the Count, he gave me a respectful bow, then turned to my lord Raimondin.

'Cousin, were you party to this plan?'

My lord Raimondin made as if to answer, but I held up my hand, motioning him to remain silent.

'By your leave, my lord Count, I give you my word that my lord Raimondin knew nothing of this. It is true that he made the request at my instruction, but he remained in complete ignorance of the plan I had formed. If I have incurred your wrath, then I most humbly beg your pardon. But please, my lord, do not hold this against your cousin. If you wish to punish anyone for this, then I alone assume full responsibility.'

The Count turned to my lord.

'Dear cousin, your intended is indeed a lady of great beauty, wisdom and cleverness. I must own that I am perchance a little vexed at this trick she has succeeded in playing upon me, but having pledged my word concerning your initial request, I am happy

to abide by it. Lay out the thread upon the ground, and such land as it may enclose will be yours.'

9

Tuesday

'Mmm, those were absolutely delicious. And served in a proper marmite pot too!'

'As good as you get in France?'

'Every bit as good! Where do they get them?' Mel reached for the bread-basket, picked up a large chunk of fresh crusty brown bread, and began soaking up the last of the *marinière* sauce. *Table manners be damned. This is what everybody would do back home.*

'They're farmed in special mussel-beds in the Menai Straits. I sometimes see the mussel-boats out there harvesting them.'

Mel thought for a moment. 'Now you mention it, I think I might have seen them. Are they the ones with flat bottoms? I thought they looked a bit odd, because they reminded me of the oyster boats we get on the Atlantic coast at home.'

Ray nodded. 'We have local oysters

too, but they're not from the Straits; they're farmed at an oyster hatchery on the island.' He tossed his last empty mussel shell into the lid of the marmite and reached for the finger-bowl. 'So, tell me a bit more about this thesis of yours. What exactly are you researching?'

Mel looked up. 'It's complicated to describe in detail, but it's mainly about French folklore. At the moment I'm concentrating on one particular medieval manuscript.'

'So why did you come here to do it?' he asked, as he rinsed the sauce from his fingers. 'Not that I'm complaining, but wouldn't it have been more logical to do it at a French university?'

'In some ways, yes, but . . .' Her voice trailed off.

'But what?'

'I'd had . . . one or two . . . problems back home. I needed to go somewhere completely different, where nobody knew me. Where I could make a completely fresh start.'

Ray dried his hands on his napkin,

then reaching across the table took hold of her free hand. 'What sort of problems?'

Mel opened her mouth to say that she didn't really want to talk about it, but closed it again without replying.

Yes, he does deserve some kind of explanation. But how little can I get away with telling him?

She drew a deep breath. 'It's a bit difficult to explain, but, basically, the problems were with my . . . ex-partner.'

'Boyfriend trouble, then?'

'Yes, I suppose you could call it that. We had a . . .' She paused, staring into her wineglass whilst searching for the right word. 'A disagreement. And I realised that I couldn't stay with him.'

Ray squeezed her hand. 'I'm so sorry.'

'And my parents had both died, so I had no reason to stay in France. I looked at the various possibilities, and I came here because . . . Well, it's a good university, I can speak English, and it just seemed like the right thing to do.' She sighed. 'I hadn't realised about Welsh, though!'

Ray chuckled. 'I shouldn't worry too much about that — Welsh people speak English as well! Both languages are taught in schools, so the children grow up bilingual. But, seriously, now that you're here, do you think it was a good idea?'

She looked up into his smouldering dark eyes, caught her breath, and smiled.

'Yes, most definitely.'

★　★　★

And so it was that my dear lord Raimondin acquired for himself the lands of Lusignan.

The other nobles of the court of Poitou had mocked him for his poverty, and continued to mock him for his lack of a castle of his own. But their complacency towards him was of but short duration, for in the brief space of one night, and using only an apronful of stones and a mouthful of water, I used my own magical powers to build for him a magnificent castle. My dearest lord named it Le Château de Lusignan, and I — who had been its creator — was given the affectionate title of La Mère de Lusignan.

A short while afterwards, our marriage took place within the castle I had erected. My lord Raimondin invited his cousins Bertram and Blaniferte to be the guests of honour at the festivities. Both were much impressed with the castle, with its furnishings, and with its lands. Our marriage ceremony was held at the hour of nine in the forenoon, and the feasting and dancing continued apace until sundown. At last our guests took their leave, and I and my lord were left alone.

In order that my lord and I might enjoy as much time together as we were able ere I should have to assume my seclusion, I requested that the ceremony might take place on a Monday. That night, as we retired to our chamber, I became fully aware for the first time how much I longed to be with him, and how difficult this repeated enforced sep-aration would be for me. The mere thought of it was sufficient to make me weep. My dear lord, seeing my tears, held me in his arms and asked me most tenderly what was troubling me.

I was silent. What, in the name of

everything I have ever held as holy, could I tell him?

'My dearest lord, do you recall the night of our first meeting?'

'My dearest lady, I will remember that night until the end of my days, for it was then that my life changed for ever.'

'It was that very same night that you asked me to become your wife.'

'Indeed it was. What of it?'

'Do you also recall that when I agreed to become your wife, it was subject to one condition?'

He gazed at me curiously.

'Why do you ask, my dearest?'

'Because, my lord, though it causes me unutterable pain, I must remind you of that condition. I told you that for one day in every seven, I must be able to spend the time from midnight on Friday until midnight on Saturday in complete seclusion. And you readily agreed. Do you recall this?'

'I recall your words, dearest wife, but I must own that I had given but little thought to them. I was so overjoyed that you had consented to be my wife that at the time I *was prepared to agree to any condition you imposed.' His face grew serious. 'Surely, my love, you are not going to insist that I continue to abide by it?'*

I turned my face away so that he should not see me weeping afresh.

'I am sorry, my lord, but I have no choice than to insist upon it. It pains me to have to do so, and it pains me even more that I may not tell you the reason. But this I can disclose: that if you — or indeed any other member of the household — should attempt to intrude upon my privacy during my period of seclusion, such an intrusion will in all certainty cause us to become separated for ever.'

By this time, I was weeping openly. My lord said nothing, but placed his hand beneath my chin and gently raised my face so that his dark eyes could look into my own. With his other hand he wiped away my tears, and brushed his lips against my burning brow.

'Dearest lady wife,' he murmured. 'I would not for the world be prepared to run the risk of losing you. Therefore, if this matter is of such great importance to you,

then I will readily agree to abide by your wishes. I give you my solemn vow that for one day in every seven, from midnight on Friday until midnight on Saturday, I will allow you to remain in total seclusion, and that neither I nor any members of our household will ever venture to intrude upon you during this period. And now I will seal this vow . . .'

I made as if to answer my thanks, but my lips were stopped by the pressure of his own upon them. This, I now knew, was the happiness which had eluded me for so long.

Later, as I lay in my lord's arms and listened to his gentle breathing as he slept, I prayed. I prayed, to whatever divine beings might listen, that this happiness which I had at last been so fortunate as to find might remain with me. The notion that in order to preserve it meant that I must go on deceiving my dearest lord was something which pained me beyond measure. But if this were the price I should have to pay to be sure of that continuing happiness, then — and may all the gods come to my aid — so be it.

10

Wednesday

Ray parked the car in Beaumaris' main car park — a vast grassy expanse at one end of the town, overlooking the Menai Straits. Mel looked around, taking in the view of the Victorian houses and the castle walls. In the middle distance she could make out the shape of a pier jutting out over the water, framed by the Snowdonia mountains in the background.

'What do you want to do first?' Ray asked.

'I've no idea! You're the one who knows the town. I'm happy to follow your lead.'

Ray thought for a moment. 'Well, the weather looks good and the sea looks nice and calm. How about starting with a Puffin Island cruise?'

'Puffin Island? What's that?'

By way of answer, Ray pointed eastwards towards a large rock rising out of the sea in the far distance. 'That. It's a bird sanctuary. The boats leave from the pier and the trip takes about an hour or so. Do you fancy that?'

Mel smiled and nodded, and they made their way towards the pier and joined the queue at the booking kiosk. As luck would have it, there was a cruise due to set off in about quarter of an hour. They walked to the far end of the pier, climbed aboard the boat and found two seats on the fore deck, just in front of the wheelhouse.

The engine started up, and the skipper made the obligatory safety announcement as the boat drew away from the pier and began its journey along the Straits.

'Why is it called Puffin Island?' Mel asked. 'Do you get puffins there?'

'Yes,' Ray answered, 'but not all the time. You won't see any puffins there at this time of year. They arrive in the spring to nest on the island, but they're all gone by mid-summer. It's called Puffin Island because it used to be a very good breeding ground for puffins.'

'Used to be? Isn't it now?'

'Well, yes, but there used to be a lot more than there are today. Apparently, pickled puffin used to be quite a delicacy. Don't look like that — I can't imagine it either! And then there was a big problem with rats, which almost wiped out the entire puffin colony. They're gradually starting to build up the numbers again now, but as I said, there aren't any there at the moment. But there are lots of other birds on the island. You'll see them in a bit.'

Mel became aware that whilst they had been talking, the skipper of the boat (a man who looked and sounded about the same age as Ray) had begun giving a commentary about the history of the town of Beaumaris and the surrounding area. The castle, clearly visible from the boat, had been built by King Edward I at the end of the thirteenth century, as part of a chain of fortifications built across North Wales following his victory over the Welsh. But unlike the other castles, this one had never been finished.

He went on to explain that the Welsh name for Puffin Island was Ynys Seiriol, which meant Seiriol's Island. Seiriol was a sixth-century Celtic saint who had founded a monastery at nearby Penmon, and was now buried on Puffin Island.

'We're now approaching Penmon Point,' the skipper went on. 'If you look over to the headland on the port side of the boat, you can see a church with a square tower. That is all that remains of St Seiriol's church, and the shorter tower to the right of it, with a domed top, is an old dovecote.'

The boat chugged past the black-and-white lighthouse which stood offshore by the eastern tip of the point, then picked up speed as it headed across the open water towards Puffin Island. As they approached, Mel became aware that what had appeared from a distance to be a large expanse of pale grey rock was in fact row upon row of grey-and-white seabirds. Her nostrils were ambushed by the sudden sharp scent of guano.

'What are those birds?' she asked.

'The pale grey-and-white ones are kittiwakes,' Ray answered. 'And those big black ones with the pale faces are cormorants.'

'Why are they sitting with their wings spread out like that?'

'They dive to catch fish, and they need to dry their feathers after they've been underwater.'

'What about the smaller black-and-white birds?'

Ray peered through his binoculars. 'If they've got white fronts and pointed beaks, they're guillemots. The ones with the black flattish-shaped beaks are razor-bills. And that big grey one over there, with a yellow beak, is a grey heron.'

As they watched, the heron pounced into the water and re-emerged with a wriggling silver shape clamped in its beak. Several of the cormorants imme-diately left their perches and mobbed the heron, trying to force it to drop its quarry. The heron took to the air and headed back towards the mainland. The cormorants gave up the chase, returned to their perches on the rocks, and spread out their wings as before.

Mel was about to speak when the tannoy crackled into life again. 'Look over to the port side,' the skipper announced. 'On the rocks just above the waterline there are three grey seals.'

Ray whistled under his breath. 'Wow, just look at those. Aren't they magnificent? And it's such a treat to see them so close.'

Mel followed his gaze. 'Are those the same kind as the one we saw on Sunday?'

'Yes. But these are much clearer. It's great to get such a good view of them.'

The boat slowed down and came to a halt as it drew level with the far end of the island. The skipper carried on with the commentary, pointing out the various seabirds which Ray had already described to Mel. She was carefully scanning the rocks, looking to identify the birds, when Ray suddenly grabbed her arm.

'Look! Over there!' He pointed out to sea.

'Where?' She looked, but could see nothing unusual.

'Just there, on the surface of the water. Porpoises!'

The skipper paused his commentary, handed the helm to his companion, then made his way to where Ray and Mel were sitting. 'Porpoises, you said?' he asked, barely able to conceal his excitement.

Ray nodded and pointed.

'How do you know they're porpoises?' asked the man who was sitting alongside them. 'They look more like dolphins to me.'

'It's all to do with size, and also the way they move through the water,' Ray explained. 'For a start, porpoises are a lot smaller than dolphins. And watch the fins on their backs. Can you see how they're sort of 'rolling' through the water, a bit like wheels? Dolphins don't move like that.'

'Would you mind taking the mike for a few minutes and explaining all that to everybody?' the skipper asked. 'I'm fairly new to this job, and I've never seen these before!'

'Well, if it helps, I'd be happy to. Mel, would you excuse me for a moment?'

'Er — yes, of course.' Mel turned her attention back to the water as Ray followed the skipper back to the bridge. A moment later, his voice came over the loudspeakers:

'Ladies and gentlemen, if you'd care to look out to the right and watch the surface of the water, you will see a group of porpoises. I know that when a lot of people see porpoises, they mistake them for dolphins. And at first sight the two do look similar, but it's easy to tell them apart once you know what you're looking for . . .'

★ ★ ★

During the months following our marriage, I contrived to increase the size of the Château de Lusignan and strengthen its fortifications. In the fullness of time, it became the fairest and strongest castle for many a long mile. It was surrounded on three sides by the

River Mère, and commanded a fine view of the countryside beyond. For myself, I constructed at one corner of the keep a tall tower with a winding staircase leading to a secure chamber at the top. The chamber was locked with a key which I kept with me at all times. I furnished the room to my own preference, with a large bed, a writing-desk and chair, and a large bathing tub. The latter would be supplied with water by a complicated mechanism involving a pulley system which linked to the underground well. This water could be heated using a copper on the fire.

This tower became the place where I spent my Saturdays in total seclusion. It was known to the castle household as the 'Tour de la Mère de Lusignan', named after the affectionate title which my dear lord had bestowed upon me. All knew that once I had retired to this tower on a Friday evening, I must never be disturbed until such time as I should emerge. Although I could have chosen to go to sleep in the tower and stay there until Sunday morning, truth to tell I could not bear the thought of spending two successive nights away from my dear lord's bed. *Accordingly, once each Saturday was over and the hour of midnight had struck, I would light a lanthorn, unlock the door, descend the stairs of the tower, and make my way to the chamber which I and my dear husband had shared since our marriage.*

The first time I had done this, my lord Raimondin was already asleep when I crept into the bed beside him, and he was not aware of my presence until he awoke with the rays of the sun on Sunday morning. The look of pure joy on his countenance, when he became aware that I was once again lying by his side, was a joy to behold. I might even go so far as to say that his smile outshone the sunlight as he took me once more into his loving arms. I told him, between his fervent kisses, that I could not bear to be separated from him for a moment longer than was absolutely essential. Accordingly, every Saturday night thereafter, my dearest lord would contrive to remain awake until the hour of midnight had passed, and eagerly await the moment soon afterwards when I could return to his loving embrace.

Within the space of a twelvemonth I had

conceived and borne our first child — a son, whom we baptised with the name of Urian. He was a healthy child and grew quickly, although his appearance was somewhat unusual. He had a large mouth and pendulous ears, and his eyes, though bright and clear, were of two wildly differing colours. The left eye was a clear shade of emerald green, but the right eye was as bright and sparkling as a pure ruby. Yet my dear lord would hear no word spoken on the matter of our son's disfigurement, and all the members of our household, including his nursemaid, knew better than to gainsay his decree.

The same was true when, after a further twelvemonth, our second son was born. To him we gave the name of Cedes. He too was healthy and strong, yet the skin of his face was as scarlet as the right eye of his elder brother.

Notwithstanding the strange matter of our sons' physical appearances, we both loved them dearly. And in token of our gratitude for their safe deliverance and continued good health, I erected and furnished an abbey in the nearby town of Malliers. I also gave some thought to building a place of residence for Cedes for when he should grow to adulthood. Urian would, of course, in the fullness of time inherit the castle of Lusignan, but I did not wish to think about the circumstances which would give rise to that. The mere thought of losing my dear lord filled my whole being with a cold sense of dread.

But forcing myself to put such dismal thoughts out of my mind, I turned my attention to the construction of a castle for Cedes. Accordingly, on the occasion of his first birthday, I made for him a fine and strong castle which became known as Favent.

Shortly after this, I gave birth to our third son. He was baptised Gyot. Like his brothers he was a fine and a healthy child, but he too had a curious disfigurement. It was not so striking as that of Urian or Cedes, but it was troubling nonetheless: the two eyes in his face were at differing levels.

He too would require his own residence when he became a grown man, and for him I constructed a fine, twin-towered fortress on the coast, at the place known as La Rochelle.

Our fourth son we named Antoine. He too was born with a strange physical deformity: he was covered from head to toe in thick coarse hair, and on his hands, in the place where his fingernails should have been, he had long sharp claws.

Our fifth son, whom we named Freimund, had but one eye.

Our sixth son we named Geoffroy. He became known as Geoffroy with the Tooth, for he had a long tooth, resembling the tusk of a boar, protruding from his jaw.

And yet, despite their various disfigurements, our sons all grew to become courageous warriors and illustrious heroes. In the fullness of time, Freimund grew weary of fighting, and announced that he wished to take holy orders.

So it was that he entered the Abbey at Malliers. It pained me a little to think that he would never know the true love which had brought so much joy to me and his father, but I forced myself to accept that if this was his chosen path, then it was no business of mine to stand in the way of his following it. On the day that he took the cowl, both I and his father said a prayer for his happiness and success in the life he had chosen.

Had we but known what was to befall our dear son so soon thereafter, we would have said many, many more.

11

Wednesday

'Thank you. That was fascinating.' Mel smiled, as they left the boat and walked back along the pier towards the town. 'I'd no idea you knew so much.'

Ray chuckled modestly. 'Well, I've studied it fairly well over the years. I even did one of my assignments on the marine life of the Menai Straits. So, how about taking a look round the castle now?'

'Ooh, yes, please. It looks amazing. I was surprised how big it was when we saw it from the boat.'

'Yes, it's pretty impressive.'

'Why was it never finished?'

'To be honest I'm not quite sure. Rumour has it that they just ran out of money. It's a shame, though. It would have been quite magnificent.'

They made their way along Castle Street, passing an impressive array of colourful shops, pubs, hotels and restaurants, and arrived at the ticket office which was discreetly incorporated into the outer wall of the castle. Ray took out his wallet and asked for two tickets.

Mel held up her hand. 'Please, Ray, let me pay for this. You paid for the boat trip. This is my treat.'

Ray made as if to protest, but Mel had already handed over a twenty-pound note.

'We've got a special Victorian event going on this week,' said the girl at the counter, as she rang the payment through the till and gave Mel her change. 'I'm afraid we've run out of copies of the programme, but there's a poster up on the wall in the main courtyard.'

'Thank you.' Mel pushed the tickets into her handbag, and the two of them wandered through into the outer ward. Nearby, in the moat, they could see a family of swans, picking up chunks of bread thrown into the water by some of the passers-by. The five cygnets were almost as large as the adult birds, but at least twice as greedy. Mel started to walk towards them, but Ray grabbed her arm and pulled her back.

'Stay well clear,' he whispered. 'The adults can get quite aggressive if they've got young. Some people reckon they're strong enough to break your arm. I'm not sure if that's true, but I wouldn't want to be the one to find out.'

Mel shuddered. 'Neither would I. OK, let's leave them alone.'

They walked through the imposing gatehouse into the inner ward of the castle. Inside was a hive of activity, featuring food-stalls and fairground-style sideshows. Ray's face lit up as he caught sight of a tall narrow booth covered in striped canvas.

'Hey, look — Punch and Judy! Come on, we've got to see this!' He grabbed Mel's hand and they ran towards the stand, arriving as the show was just starting. Mel peered at the puppets cavorting on the small stage, then her face cleared into a broad smile.

'Ah yes — *Le Spectacle de Guignol*! That's what we call this in France.'

They found a place to stand at the back of the crowd, and leaned together against the wall to watch the rest of the show. The children in the audience chuckled with glee as Mr Punch constantly outwitted all the other characters, and roared with delight at the appearance of the sausage-stealing crocodile.

'I think they must have cleaned the story up since I last saw it,' Mel whispered into Ray's ear, careful not to let the children hear her. 'Punch isn't nearly as violent to Judy in this version. And what's happened to the bit where he kills the baby?'

'I don't know,' Ray whispered back. 'It's a long time since I saw a Punch & Judy show, but I do remember that. And it looks as though they've got rid of the part with the hangman, too. But then, I don't suppose that would make much sense to today's audience.'

Mel nodded. 'It's probably better that way,' she murmured, as the two of them joined in the applause as the puppets took their bows.

Next door to the Punch & Judy Show was another much larger booth, labelled *The Palace of Curiosities*. Outside was a cheery-looking man dressed in dark trousers, maroon double-breasted waistcoat, starched white shirt with floral cravat, beige frock-coat and black top hat. As they approached, he removed his hat and swept a low bow.

'Greetings, sir, madame! May I bid you welcome to the amazing, astounding, incredible Palace of Curiosities!'

Ray returned the theatrical bow. 'Greetings, good sir!'

Mel stifled a chuckle.

'You see before you,' the proprietor went on, 'a unique collection, dating back hundreds — if not thousands — of years, of the most incredible curiosities of nature. All are gathered together here in one place, for your delight, delectation, entertainment and amusement. Please, allow me to give you a guided tour!'

'It would be our pleasure, sir!' Ray grinned, entering fully into the charade.

114

'Please continue!'

'The pleasure, good sir, is all mine. Pray, follow me!' The proprietor led them into the booth and made his way towards the back, stopping in front of a large object covered with a pair of curtains. He drew back one of them, exposing the left-hand half of a tall glass-fronted cabinet, then pointed to a small, glass-topped container on the top shelf. It contained what appeared to be a white linen cloth covered with small black spots.

'This,' he explained, 'is a collection of taxidermied fleas from all around the world. Many of them used to perform in flea circuses, and after they died they were carefully preserved, in homage to their great talents. Next to this,' (he indicated a small, shapeless blackened object about two inches long) 'we have the other ear of Vincent Van Gogh — the one which he did not sever during his lifetime.'

Ray gasped in mock horror.

'You may well be shocked, good sir!' the proprietor exclaimed. 'But wait until you see what we have on the shelf below!

115

Have you heard of the sad tale of Hans Brinker?'

Ray and Mel both shook their heads.

'Hans Brinker was a Dutch boy who lived by the canals of the Low Countries. The landscape was protected by raised banks called dykes, and one cold dark winter's night one of those dykes began to leak. Young Hans, walking past, noticed the leak, realised that the village would flood, so placed his finger in the hole to stop the leak. All night he stayed there, bravely plugging the hole with his finger, but unable to leave and call for help. The next morning the villagers found his cold, stiff little body, still with his finger plugging the hole in the dyke. His brave action had saved the village, but alas, only at the cost of his own short life. This . . .' He paused as he pointed to another blackened object, the size and shape of a wrinkled chipolata sausage. 'This is that very finger!'

'Really?' Ray asked.

'Really! As real as the object next to it. This is the horn of a unicorn. For

116

centuries, it was stored in the crypt of Nôtre Dame cathedral in Paris!'

Mel glanced at Ray and raised her eyebrows. Fortunately, the proprietor appeared not to have noticed, as he was already turning his attention to the two objects which occupied the bottom shelf of the cupboard.

'And here, we have two dolls from the Belgian Congo. One of them is from the Bushongo tribe and the other from the Bakongo tribe, both of whom believed that they were powerful talismans which could ward off evil spirits. The dolls were recently found in a disused warehouse in Southampton, and it is said that they were destined to travel on the *Titanic*. Who knows — if they had been taken on board, the ship might well not have floundered! They also have great potency as fertility dolls, and for this reason we advise ladies not to gaze too long at them. We cannot accept any responsibility for any unforeseen consequences!'

Mel and Ray both chuckled as the

proprietor drew back the other curtain. The right-hand half of the cabinet had no intermediate shelves, and contained just one item: a painted figurine about two feet high. It looked like a miniature version of an Egyptian mummy-case.

'This,' he explained, 'is a *Shabti*. Their purpose was to carry out heavy manual tasks in the afterlife. This particular one is made in the likeness of Queen Cleopatra, and is highly prized — for reasons which I shall now reveal!'

Ray and Mel gave appreciative nods, then winked at each other as the proprietor turned briefly away from them to lift the figure out of the cabinet. He laid it down carefully on a small table, pausing for dramatic effect before removing the top section.

'This *Shabti* was made to house the mummified hand of the great Queen of the Nile herself!'

Ray and Mel both let out loud gasps. In Mel's case, the gasp was only partially for show. The sight of the bandage-wrapped artefact was something she

118

found inexplicably shocking. Truth to tell, the whole episode was making her feel distinctly uneasy. Who on earth was this strange man, and how had he managed to acquire such a bizarre collection of oddities?

Ray, however, still appeared to be playing along. 'That is truly amazing!' he declared, in mock solemnity.

'Indeed it is, good sir!' the proprietor answered. 'But that is not all! If you look closely at the *Shabti*, you will notice something very unusual. If, as many believe, this is a true likeness of Queen Cleopatra, then it would appear that she had not two but three arms!'

He pointed to one side of the figure. True enough, close examination revealed that it had a second left arm.

'Really?' Ray exclaimed. 'How extraordinary! How on earth do you know all this?'

'Ah, good sir, thereby hangs a very long tale — and if I were to embark upon the telling of it, we should all remain here for many more hours to come!

Suffice it to say that when I acquired this extraordinary artefact, following the sudden and unexplained death of its previous owner, it came with a detailed history dating back many years. It contains many strange claims. Some even say that the object is cursed!'

'Cursed?' Mel shuddered.

'Aye, fair lady! But I for one set no store by such wild accusations. What truth can there possibly be in the idea that bad fortune can be invoked simply by uttering a few ill-chosen words?'

Mel's eyes widened. 'What indeed,' she murmured, as she watched him replace the lid on the *Shabti* and return it to the cabinet.

'Unfortunately,' he went on, 'I have been unable to bring some of the palace's other curiosities to this exhibition today. Had I more space, I could have shown you the mummified head of an ancient Peruvian Emperor, lovingly preserved in cocoa. Or the two-headed pig from Peking, taken from the Chinese Emperor's summer palace by the

99th Foot Regiment during the Second Opium War. Or the Windermere Monster — caught by rod and line in Lake Windermere, and somewhat larger and more impressive than its better-known Scottish cousin. But now, if you care to step this way, I can show you what is perhaps the most exciting exhibit in the whole of the Palace of Curiosities!'

He led them across to the other side of the booth, stopping in front of what appeared to be an ordinary two-wheeled handcart, of the sort previously used by street-sellers. It was painted bright red, and on top of the platform was a box-like shape covered with a heavy red velvet cloth. Taking hold of one corner, he turned to face them as he continued his spiel.

'Way back in 1884, the crew of *HMS Galatea* dropped anchor at Marcus Island in the Pacific Ocean, two hundred miles south-west of Japan. It was here that they encountered and captured a creature never before seen — and which provided absolute proof of Charles

Darwin's theory that man is descended from fish. Madame, sir, I give you —THE MARCUS ISLAND MERMAID!'

Mel's jaw dropped open as he whisked away the velvet covering, revealing a wooden box, about four feet long and about a foot high. One long side of the box had been replaced by a glass panel, through which was visible a grotesque mummified creature.

'The sailors of *HMS Galatea* placed the creature in a barrel of rum to preserve it for the voyage home', the proprietor went on. 'But, sailors being sailors, they could not resist the lure of the rum, and by the time they finally reached England, less than half of the liquor was left. Which is why the mermaid is only half-preserved!'

Mel and Ray both stared at the creature, which occupied the whole length of the box, in undisguised amazement. From the waist downwards there was an unmistakable smooth and shiny fishtail, but the part above the waist was wizened and desiccated — supposedly human, but consisting of taut yellow skin stretched over bulging, mis-shapen ribs, stick-thin arms and gnarled hands, and a hideous, hairless skull. The face, such as it was, had sunken cheeks and a wide jaw set in a rictus grin.

It was Ray who recovered first. He forced his face back into a smile and resumed the role of the fascinated spectator.

'That is truly amazing! A genuine mermaid?'

The proprietor beamed. 'Sir, the evidence is before you!' He turned to Mel. 'Madame, what do you think?'

Mel's eyes remained fixed on the contents of the box.

'*C'est incroyable,*' she said truthfully, when she finally found her voice. 'I have never, ever, seen anything like that.'

★ ★ ★

In the fullness of time, my husband's ageing father, the Comte de la Forêt, left his lowly home and came to live with us in the castle.

My dear lord Raimondin also took care of the needs of his brothers; to all of them, he made the generous gifts of money so that they might at last acquire their own homes and live out their lives in dignity and comfort.

One night, as I rejoined my dear lord in our bedchamber after the four and twenty hours of my seclusion had elapsed, he seemed troubled.

'What ails you, my lord?' I asked.

He hesitated before answering me, 'Dearest lady, this evening, whilst we were at dinner, my father enquired of me why you are never seen on Saturdays.'

This troubled me greatly, but I made answer as lightly as I could. 'Indeed, my lord? And what did you give by way of answer?'

Thankfully, he appeared not to have perceived my alarm.

'Truth to tell, my dearest, I did not know what answer I should give, save that your desire to spend your Saturdays in seclusion was a request to which I agreed and which I have never questioned. I told him that I did not consider it to be any concern of mine.' He

paused, then his handsome face broke into a slow smile. 'Indeed, my dearest, I hoped that by saying this, I might also convey to him the notion that not only was it no concern of mine, but also that it should be no concern of his.'

'Thank you, my lord,' I murmured, as I crept into his waiting arms. 'I am most fortunate to have such a kind and understanding husband. Indeed, oft I think that I am not worthy of you.'

'Dearest lady,' he murmured into my hair, 'it is I who am not worthy of you. I never cease to be astounded that you should have chosen me as your lord. You are wise, kind, intelligent and beautiful. Indeed, you are as fair today as on that fateful night in the forest so long ago, when I first set eyes upon you.'

As I felt his arms tighten around me, I hid my face against his shoulder, in order that my countenance should not betray my fear.

My dreadful secret had remained safe for more than two decades, during which time my dear lord had never once attempted to *discover or question it. Oh, how I wished, with every fibre of my being, that I should not have to go on deceiving him.*

But now I began to wonder: for how much longer would this happiness go on, now that others were beginning to question my secret?

12

Wednesday

'You look miles away.' Ray's voice dragged Mel out of her reverie.

They had left the hubbub of activity in the courtyard and had climbed up through passages inside the thick castle walls, eventually reaching the accessible part of the battlements. The wall walk offered a commanding view along Castle Street in one direction, and across the Menai Straits in the other.

Mel, who had been staring out thoughtfully over the water, turned round to face him.

'I was thinking about that mermaid. Do people really believe that it's real?'

Ray grinned. 'Of course not. Well, not nowadays, anyway. Though I can't speak for what might have happened in the past. Judging by the popularity of that sort of freak show in Victorian times, maybe people used to be a lot more easily taken in by them.'

'Freak show?'

Ray nodded. 'That's basically what they were. The Victorians were very strait-laced and narrow-minded, and were very suspicious of anything even remotely out of the ordinary. So their idea of a freak could have been something as simple as someone who was extremely tall or extremely short. Sometimes people like that were shunned by polite society, so they could only scratch a living by appearing in freak shows. The shows appealed to a certain type of morbid curiosity.'

'Really?' Mel shuddered. 'But what about the mermaid?'

Ray laughed. 'That 'mermaid'' (he made imaginary inverted commas in the air with his fingers) 'was made up of the top half of a monkey sewed on to the tail of a fish. It was a common trick. That creature we saw down there was a particularly fine example, but it's no more a mermaid than you or I! Everyone knows there's no such thing as mermaids.'

Mel considered. 'A common trick? How common?'

'You'd be surprised. Once people had heard the stories about mermaids, some crafty sailors decided to try to make money out of the idea. They'd make fake mermaids in the way I just said. There was plenty of opportunity whilst they were out on their travels. They'd find a dead monkey of some sort, take the top half, which looked vaguely human, then catch a fish and sew its tail on to the bottom. Then they'd leave the whole thing to dry out. By the time they got back to England, they had a pretty convincing-looking mummified specimen which easily fooled gullible people who didn't know any better. I've seen quite a few of them in museums, but I must admit they weren't usually as big as that one we saw just now.'

Mel turned back towards the Straits and stared out to sea. 'But I don't understand,' she said eventually. 'If, as you say, mermaids don't exist, then why did people appear to believe in them?'

'Seals.'

'What?'

'Did you notice the way the seals were lying on the rocks when we saw them from the boat? They've got huge eyes, so in poor light their faces look as though they could be human, and their flippers could easily be mistaken for arms. The fish's tail just adds to the illusion.'

'So . . .'

'Yes. Just imagine it. The poor sailors have been out at sea for months on end, and by that stage they've probably almost forgotten what women even look like. Then, they see the rocks in the distance, and on the top there are these shapes which look for all the world like women with fishes' tails. The sailors' imaginations, and their frustrations, go into overdrive. When they get home, they tell stories about these wonderful creatures they've seen — half-woman, half-fish — and gullible people believe them.'

Mel turned back to face him. 'What an amazing story. I never knew that about seals.'

'Well, I think they were actually man-atees — a particular type of seal which is only found in the tropics. It's claimed that Columbus saw some on one of his voyages, and recorded them as being mermaids. That probably helped to fuel the legend.'

Mel glanced down into the court-yard, where the Palace of Curiosities was doing a roaring trade.

'Just a legend, then?'

Ray grinned and laid a reassuring arm around her shoulders. 'Of course. And now, how about looking round the rest of the castle?'

★ ★ ★

It was a little after a twelvemonth after this episode that we were struck by the disaster which was to cause the dreadful catastro-phe, and end my years of happiness with my dearest lord.

One morning, a messenger arrived in great haste at the gates of the Château de Lusignan. He insisted on speaking to the Lord Raimondin face to face. My lord summoned me to his side as the messenger addressed us:

'My lord, it is with a heavy heart that I bring you dire tidings. Your son, Geoffroy with the Tooth, has raised an army and has attacked the Abbey of Malliers. Yesternight, he burned the abbey to the ground, and all therein have perished.'

'All therein?' I asked, in a voice which I did not recognise as my own.

'Ay, my lady, all. The abbot and all the monks.'

'Did Geoffroy with the Tooth not know,' my lord gasped, 'that amongst those monks was his own brother Freimund?'

'That I know not, my lord,' the messenger answered, in a voice which trembled with fear. Clearly, the man was afraid that my lord would be angry with him for being the bearer of such dreadful tidings.

My lord Raimondin turned to the messenger.

'Good sir,' he said, speaking with as much dignity as he could muster, 'I thank you for bringing us this news. Although the tidings are dire, their nature cannot be blamed upon the one who has brought them. Please, leave us now and return to your duties.'

'Thank you, my lord.' The messenger gave a low bow and took his leave. As the door closed behind him, my lord turned to me. In his eyes was an expression which I had never before seen, and one which filled me with fear and foreboding. It was not an expression of grief or sorrow, but rather one of hatred and fury.

'What ails you, my dear lord?' I ventured to ask him.

I laid my hand upon his arm, but he dashed it away so violently that I was knocked aside. I looked up into his eyes, but saw in them naught but loathing.

'My lord,' I whispered. 'Pray, tell me: what have I done to offend you?'

By way of answer, he towered over me, his face dark and menacing, and spat: 'Away, you vile creature! You have contaminated my noble race!'

I made as if to answer, but instead I fell to the floor and blessed blackness descended upon me. When I next opened my eyes, my

dear lord was kneeling at my side and crad-
ling me in his arms.

'Dearest lady, please forgive me for having spoken to you so cruelly.'

'You are forgiven, my lord,' I answered.
'But please tell me, what made you speak to
me so harshly?'

He opened his mouth to reply, but no
words emerged. Instead, he drew me closer to
him. I could feel his arms trembling around
me, and could hear his heart pounding as I
laid my head upon his shoulder.

'My lord?'

I looked up, my eyes misted by my tears,
and saw that he too was weeping. When he
did finally answer, his voice faltered . . .

13

Friday

Passing the café on her way back from the shops, Mel paused and smiled to herself. Was it really only a week since she'd first been here, and had met the lovely Ray? She decided, on a whim, to call in and say hello. There was no obvious sign of Ray, but Myfanwy was standing behind the counter. Mel couldn't help thinking that she looked tired and drained. Remembering what Ray had told her a couple of days ago, Mel gave her a friendly smile.

'Good morning, Myfanwy. Is Ray around?'

'No, sorry, love, he's out at the moment. And I'm not sure what time he'll be back. He left in a great hurry and didn't say how long he would be. Do you want to wait, or would you rather come back later?'

'I'll wait for a little while, if that's all

right. It was starting to rain just as I came in, so I don't really want to go out again just yet.'

'Would you like a drink whilst you're waiting?'

'Yes, please.' Mel peered up at the blackboard. It was a little less incomprehensible now than it had been on her first visit, but there was still a bewildering amount of choice. She settled eventually for a double espresso, this being the nearest thing she had yet found to the small strong black coffee of her homeland. Myfanwy made the coffee then moved to the till.

'One pound ninety-five, please.'

Mel handed over a five-pound note and Myfanwy counted out four pounds and five pence into her hand. Mel was on the point of putting it back in her purse when she noticed the error.

'I'm sorry, but I think you've given me too much change.' She handed back the extra pound, picked up her coffee and turned to make her way to a table, but her attention was caught by the sound of a muffled sob. She turned back to the counter to see Myfanwy holding her hand to her eyes.

'I hope you don't mind me asking, but are you all right?'

Myfanwy lowered her hand and opened her mouth to reply, but no words came out. Instead, her lip trembled and her eyes began to fill up with tears.

'Here.' Mel rummaged in her bag and pulled out a small packet of tissues. 'What's wrong? Please tell me. I might be able to help.'

'I very much doubt it, love. I don't think anyone can help with this.'

'Try me. It might help even just to talk about it. What is the phrase you use? '*A trouble shared is a trouble halved*'?'

Myfanwy dabbed at her brimming eyes. 'Oh Mel, I'm so sorry. I'm usually OK until people start being nice to me, then that just starts me off. You must think I'm such a fool.'

'Not at all.' Mel waited as the other woman wiped away a stray tear. 'Do you want to talk about it? I'll understand if you don't, but please believe me, I really want to help. Is there somewhere private we could go?'

Myfanwy shook her head sadly. 'No, I'm on my own at the moment so I can't leave the counter.' She glanced nervously around. 'But we've got the place to ourselves at the moment.' Even so, she lowered her voice to a whisper before continuing.

'You probably won't believe this,' she began.

Mel smiled. 'Let me be the judge of that. I've come across a lot of pretty unbelievable things in my time.' She reached over and patted Myfanwy's hand. To her surprise, Myfanwy clutched her hand and gripped it tightly, before drawing a deep breath and starting to speak. Once she had begun, the words tumbled out as though there was no filter between her brain and her mouth.

'It all started just over ten years ago. My son was called for jury service. Everyone was quite surprised as he was only just nineteen, and, to be honest, he was a bit nervous about it because he thought everyone else on there would be a lot older and more knowledgeable. Wordly-wise, I suppose you'd call it. Anyway, he went ahead and did it, and he was put on a case which turned out to be dangerous driving. A guy had been talking on his phone and hadn't been looking at the road, and he ran over and killed a cyclist. It was a strange case because even the Defence Counsel couldn't dispute the fact that the driver had done it, but the defence was that he hadn't been talking, he'd been dictating a voice memo. Anyway, it turned out that out of the twelve on the jury, William — that's my son — was one of only two people who could drive. So he and the other person were the only ones who understood anything about the circumstances, or could make any kind of informed decision about it. I don't know all the ins and outs of the case because William wasn't allowed to talk about it in detail. All he would say was the guy was definitely as guilty as hell, but he and the other driver had a devil of a job convincing the rest of the jury. For some reason, the Defence Counsel had managed to convince them that because the driver hadn't actually been making a phone call, it somehow weakened the case for the prosecution. The original charge was 'Causing Death by Dangerous Driving', and he wanted it reduced to 'Driving Without Due Care and Attention'.'

She paused for breath, and Mel took the opportunity to ask, 'So, what happened?'

'William and the other driver eventually managed to persuade the other people on the jury that the main point was that the man had his phone in his hand at the time, was speaking into it, and he'd taken his eye off the road and hadn't seen the cyclist, even though the visibility was good and the road was dry. So in the end they all agreed, and the guy was found guilty and sent to prison.'

'And this was — ten years ago, you said?'

Myfanwy nodded. 'Anyway, a couple

of weeks ago we realised that he's due to be released some time pretty soon. And now, William is scared stiff that he will come after him and look for revenge.'

'Revenge?' Mel frowned. 'Revenge for what?'

'For swaying the jury.' Myfanwy shuddered. 'Have you heard that saying: *A mother is only ever as happy as her least happy child*? Well, that's me right now. And it's been affecting my work here too. Like just now, when I gave you the wrong change. I'm sorry, and I know I've let everyone down, but I've been worried sick.'

Mel put her arm round her shoulders. 'Myfanwy, I'm so sorry. But tell me, please, how will this man know what you have just told me?'

'I don't understand.'

'Well, isn't the jury supposed to consult in secret?'

'Yes, but . . .' Her voice trailed off.

'So how will the man know that it was your son who convinced the other members of the jury that he was guilty? And even if he does, how will he know where to find your son? Or even who he is?'

Myfanwy looked up in surprise. 'What makes you say that?'

'Forgive me asking, but what is your family name?'

'Jones. Why?'

'Well, isn't Jones a very common name in Wales?'

Myfanwy stared at her, open-mouthed. 'You mean . . . ?'

'Yes. Even if the man knows your son's name — and there is no reason to suggest that he would — how many hundreds, or even thousands, of young men must there be who are called William Jones?'

Myfanwy's face broke into a tearful but relieved smile. 'Oh Mel, thank you so much. You have made me feel so much better. Dare I say it — you're very young, but you have wisdom well beyond your years.'

Mel felt her own smile fading, but she forced it back. 'Thank you. It's very kind of you to say so, but I'm glad I could help.'

Oh Myfanwy, what wouldn't I give to have a name as common as Jones? But you're right — revenge is a terrible thing. And as for being wise beyond my years — well, if only you knew . . .

★ ★ ★

'So that's what's been troubling her?' Ray said, after Mel had filled him in with the details later that day. 'Geez, no wonder she's been acting out of character. The poor woman must have been at her wits' end.'

Mel nodded. 'I don't know if what I said will make any difference, but she seemed to think it helped.' She frowned. 'Have you ever been on a jury?'

'Once, a couple of years ago. But I didn't get any interesting cases. You're on call for a minimum of two weeks, and for most of that time I just sat around in the waiting area, bored out of my mind doing crosswords and Sudoku puzzles. Then, on the last afternoon, I got called for a trial of someone who'd been caught

143

with cannabis. He denied it, but there was tons of evidence to prove that he was guilty. The whole trial only lasted about an hour and a half in total. If the guy had had the decency to plead Guilty in the first place, we could all have been saved a lot of trouble.' He paused. 'How about you?'

'No, never. It must be an awful responsibility, though.'

'Quite. One of my friends ended up on a jury for a murder trial. He told me afterwards that he was very glad we don't have the death penalty any more.'

'What made him say that?' Mel asked. 'Not that I'm in favour of it,' she added hastily.

'I asked him the same question,' Ray answered. 'And he said that even though it was clear that the guy in the dock was guilty, if we'd still had the death penalty he would have had a lot more difficulty in returning a *Guilty* verdict.'

'Really? Why was that?'

'He said it's not the job of the State to take that sort of revenge. And also because he'd have to spend the rest of his own life knowing that he'd sent another man to his death. And who would want to live with that on their conscience? It's odd, though, because up until then, I'd always got the impression, from things he'd said, that he'd been in favour of bringing back hanging. It's funny how circumstances alter cases.'

Mel nodded thoughtfully. 'Mmm. Yes . . . It's interesting what he said about revenge, though. I think that's what's been worrying Myfanwy. Some people do seem to believe they can take matters into their own hands . . .'

'What a gloomy subject we've got on to. Let's talk about something more cheerful.' Ray beamed. 'I have some news!'

'Oh yes? Good news, I hope?'

'Most definitely. That boat trip we went on the other day, where we saw the porpoises . . .'

'What about it?'

'After the skipper asked me to explain about the porpoises to the other passengers, he gave me his card and asked me to ring him. When I rang him, he said he wanted me to go and have a talk with him.'

'Is that where you were this morning?'

'Yes. And guess what — he wants me to go and work for him!'

'What?'

'Yes! Apparently he wants to set up a small, family-run sea-life centre, special-ising in local marine life from the Menai Straits and the coast around Anglesey. He's been thinking about it for a while, but hasn't found anyone to run it. Until now.'

'So — you'd be in charge of it, then?'

'Well, yes and no. He'd be the owner, but I would be the manager. Just imagine, Mel — this is everything I've always wanted. And I won't even have to move away from here!'

'Where would it be?'

'Just on the edge of Beaumaris. There's a perfect site there. In fact we saw it from the boat the other day, though I didn't realise it at the time. It's an old building which is pretty derelict at the moment, but he's arranging to have it kitted out with tanks, aquariums and all sorts. I think there might even be a café too.' He grinned. 'At least I'll know how to serve the customers decent coffee!'

'Ray, that's wonderful news.' She hugged him. 'Do you have any idea when it will start?'

'Not exactly, but the aim is to have it up and running by the time the main tourist season starts next Easter. That gives us about six months or so to get everything sorted. In the meantime, how about going out to celebrate?'

'Ooh, yes please. When did you have in mind?'

'Well, I can't do tonight as I'm on the late shift at the café — I had to swap with one of the others so that I could go to that interview this morning. But tomorrow should be OK.'

Oh Hell. Mel turned her face away, under the guise of looking for something in her handbag. *Tomorrow is Saturday. How on earth can I get out of this one?*

She forced herself to smile as she

looked back at him. There was no mistaking the message in those dark, shining eyes. She felt herself go weak at the knees.

She drew a deep breath. 'Ray, I'm so sorry — I can't manage tomorrow. I've . . . er . . . got something else I need to take care of.'

Ray frowned. 'Why not? Even if you're busy during the day, I bet whatever it is you're doing won't take all day AND all evening. We could still go out for a meal in the evening. Do you fancy going back to that place which does the mussels?'

Mel opened her mouth to decline, but what came out was, 'Yes, that would be lovely.'

The head says no, but the heart makes its own decisions . . .

Ray's handsome face broke into a broad smile. 'That's great. I'll book the table for seven, and pick you up about half past six.'

'OK, fine,' Mel answered, desperately hoping that she sounded more enthusiastic than she felt.

What, in the name of all that is holy, am

148

I supposed to do now? I guess I'll just have to go along with it for the moment, then some time during the day I'll call him and tell him I'm ill and can't make it. Goodness knows, I've told him enough lies already — what difference will one more make?

Ray shrugged. 'Right. I suppose I'd better get back to work. See you tomorrow.'

'Yes . . .'

Mel gave him a last quick kiss then made her way back home. Once indoors, she kicked off her shoes and slumped on to the sofa. The tears, which she had been fighting back for so long, now sprung to her eyes. She leaned forward, put her head in her hands, and sobbed like a child.

It's no use. I can't go on deceiving him like this. He thinks he knows me so well, but — shit, he doesn't even know my real name! I'm sure he still thinks I'm called Melanie. Rearrange those letters, and you get 'MEAN LIE'. How appropriate is that?

It's going to break my heart as well as his, but I'm going to have to end it, now, before he finds out the truth . . .

149

14

Saturday

As before, Mel made sure that she kept to the privacy of her own en-suite room. Fortunately, the other students who shared the house with her rarely surfaced before early afternoon on Saturdays in any case, and she was fairly confident that none of them would take any notice of her absence. She made herself as comfortable as possible, then picked up her phone and dialled Ray's number. Her heart hammered in her ears as she waited for him to pick up.

'Mel? What's up?'

She cleared her throat. 'I'm sorry, Ray, but I think I'm going to have to cancel this evening. I'm not feeling at all well.'

'In what way?'

'I'm not sure,' she lied. 'I just . . . don't feel right. I'm, sort of, cold and shivery. I don't think I'd be very good company. And I certainly wouldn't do justice to a meal out.'

'That's a shame. Will you be OK tomorrow, do you think?'

'Difficult to say at the moment. I'll let you know. In the meantime, don't arrange anything.'

'OK. Hope you start to feel better soon. I'll ring you tomorrow.'

'Thanks.' She ended the call and lay back, staring up at the ceiling through brimming eyes.

How on earth did I get myself into this mess? And why? I knew from the start that it could only end in tears. When I came here I promised myself it would be different. I had it all planned out perfectly. It was going to be a completely fresh start: no complications, no involvement, and nobody who knows anything about what's gone before. I could just let myself be me, and hope that every-one who met me would just take me at face value, without any preconceptions or preju-dices. So long, of course, as I could carry on hiding the truth.

That must have lasted all of a week and a half. I was doing fine — or so I thought — and then I met Ray. What is the phrase to describe it? Coup de foudre — a thunderclap. I thought I'd been in love before, but it was never like this. And that made me stupid enough to think that this time I might be able to make it work.

But it's just the same as it has always been — and I was a fool to believe that it could ever be otherwise. I know I can't stay here now. I'll sleep for as long as I can today, then as soon as it's midnight I'll pack up and leave. I'm sure the others will find someone else to take over my room, but all the same I'll leave some money to cover the rent. I can probably afford it more than they can.

Oh Ray, I just wish I'd had the courage to tell you how much I love you. Now you will never know. But maybe, after all, that's for the best. You'll be far better off without me. Forget me. Find someone else. Someone normal, with no dark and troubled secrets . . .

She drifted off to sleep, but the troubles didn't leave her. Her confused brain transported her back to the medieval world of the old manuscript. In her dream, she was running through the forest, trying desperately to escape from the monster which was chasing her. She stumbled and fell, then heard a voice calling her name. She looked up, and there was Ray, running towards her with his arms outstretched. But as soon as she tried to stand up and run to him, the monster caught up with her and pulled her down. She was sinking, down, down, down, into a bottomless pool of darkness. She could still hear the voice calling, 'Mel . . . Mel . . . Mel . . .' but it was growing fainter and fainter . . .

. . . then louder and louder. She eased her eyes open then realised that the voice was coming from outside the door.

'Mel, you'll have to let me in. I must see you. I'm worried about you . . .'

And then the door crashed open.

★ ★ ★

'Dearest lady, do you recall the time, when you returned to me one night, that my father had expressed his curiosity over your regular seclusion?'

'I do, my lord. It was a little over a year since, was it not?'

'Indeed it was. And I told you at the time that I had said to my father that I deemed that the matter was your own business, and therefore was no concern of mine.'

'I recall that also, my lord. And I remain eternally grateful to you for your understanding and discretion.'

He shuddered, then murmured something in a voice so low that I could not discern the words.

When I asked him to repeat what he had said, he replied, 'You should not be.'

At these words, my grief was mingled with a growing sense of alarm.

'Why not, my lord?' I whispered, hoping that my voice should not betray my fear. 'I have never had any occasion to doubt your integrity.'

'Alas, dearest lady, I am so unworthy of you.' His last words were lost in a racking sob.

'Why do you believe that, my lord?' I asked. Despite my own inner turmoil, I tried to prevent my voice from wavering.

'Because, dearest wife, I have broken my word to you.'

I shuddered. I feared that I already knew what he was about to say to me . . .

15

Saturday

'Ray? What on earth are you doing here? And how did you get in?'

'The door wasn't locked. Mel, is this some kind of sick joke?' He was standing in the bathroom doorway, staring at her in obvious disgust. 'You ring me up and tell me you can't come out this evening because you're not feeling well, when in fact you're reclining in your bathtub in some weird fancy dress costume? Why? Who are you waiting for? Some crazy guy with a fish fetish?'

'Ray, I'm so sorry. I wanted to tell you the truth — I really did. But I knew you'd never believe me —'

'The truth about what, Mel? I don't understand. Why are you lying here dressed like a mermaid?'

★   ★   ★

'I made my way to the room where you spend your days in seclusion,' my lord continued. 'The door was barred, but on putting my eye to the keyhole I was able to observe the room beyond. I could see that the room contained a bathtub, and I could see also that you were installed in the bath. At first it did not occur to me that I might be intruding upon your privacy, for as you have shared my bed these past twenty years or more, I know every inch of your fair form. Or so I had believed, until that moment.'

He paused, and looked at me through eyes brimming with sadness.

'Yet, as you turned in the water, I could see that although your upper body was always as I had known and loved, the part of you below your waist was transformed into a great scaled tail, such as that of a fish or a serpent. And yet, not three hours later, you had returned to me in your lovely human form, bearing no sign that anything untoward had befallen you. So strong was my desire to believe that nothing had happened, I forced myself to believe that the whole scene had been conjured up by my own wild imagination. And so it was that for the past twelve months I have resolutely refused to believe what I saw that fateful night; so much so that I eventually came to convince myself that it had all been naught but a ghastly nightmare.'

'Would you prefer to believe that, my lord?'

'Indeed I should, my dearest lady. And fain would I have gone on believing it, until the moment when the news reached us of the disaster at the Abbey of Malliers. For it was then that I recalled the other rumours —'

'What other rumours?' I asked, my voice sharp with fear.

'One of my brothers had told me, in confidence, that our great good fortune had given rise to many unkind comments — not least, I fear, from my cousin Bertram. In particular, it is asked, why have you remained so fair, and why has your beauty not diminished with the passing years? And why, despite your great beauty, have all of our children been born with such strange physical deformities?'

I was silent as I absorbed the full import of his words. I knew now what I must do, *although I knew also that it would mean the end of our time together.*

'My dearest lord,' I began, 'I know now that the time for secrets and deceit is over. And though it pains me beyond measure — for I know that, after this, everything will change for ever — the time is now come for me to tell you the whole truth.'

We seated ourselves side by side and I took hold of his hand. This was in part because I wanted to draw strength and comfort from its warmth as I told my dreadful tale, and also in part because I knew that after this day, never again would I have the occasion to hold it . . .

16

Saturday

'Shhh!' Mel hissed. 'The others will hear you.' She lowered her voice to a whisper. 'Please, come in and close the door, and I promise I will tell you everything. If, after that, you don't want to see me again, I will understand. But please give me the chance to explain.'

Ray hesitated, then closed the bathroom door behind him, walked across to a stool next to the wash basin, and sat down. For a few moments, neither of them spoke.

Ray eventually broke the silence. 'Well?'

'Ray, I know this is going to sound incredible. But I swear, by everything that I have ever held as holy, that every word of it is true.'

The expression on Ray's face told her that he was going to need a lot of convincing. This did not improve her courage, but she struggled to a sitting position and looked directly into his eyes.

'Well, for a start — there's the matter of my name.'

'What about it?'

'You started out thinking it was Melanie, and I was happy to let you go on believing that. You asked me a few times what Mel stood for, and you might remember that I never actually answered the question. But my name isn't Melanie. Or Melissa. Or anything like that. It's Melusine.'

'Melusine? That's an unusual name, sure enough — but why didn't you tell me?'

'Because if I did, you might work out exactly who I am.'

Ray frowned. 'What's so odd about that? And why didn't you want me to know?'

'Because I knew that if you found out the truth, you wouldn't want to know me any more. That's what happened last time . . .'

'Last time? Oh, you mean with that

boyfriend you mentioned?'

Mel nodded. 'Well, yes ... But he wasn't my boyfriend.' She paused, then drew a deep breath before adding, 'He was my husband.'

'WHAT??? You're married?'

'I was, but not any longer.'

'What happened? Where is your husband now? Is he still in France?'

Mel shook her head sadly. 'He's dead. A long time ago.'

Ray stared at her, speechless. But whether this was with anger, or shock, or horror, she couldn't tell. She reached for the glass of water on the table next to the bath, took a cautious sip, then continued.

'Perhaps I should begin at the beginning. I know it's going to sound crazy — impossible, even — but please stay and hear me out ...'

★ ★ ★

'My lord,' I began, 'do you recall the night we first met, by the fountain in the forest?'

'I do,' he answered earnestly. 'What of it?'

'Do you remember what I told you about myself?'

He paused to recollect.

'You said that you had great wealth and magical powers.'

'Did it not occur to you to wonder why I should have magical powers?'

He shook his head sadly. 'No, dearest lady, it did not. I was so entranced by your beauty and charm — indeed, my love, I still am — that I had but one thought: that you should be mine. If you would agree to be my wife, I was prepared to accept you as you were, without question.'

I looked up at him, my eyes blinded by unshed tears.

'It is the fact that you were prepared to accept me as I was, without question, which has meant that we could be together. But alas, that can no longer be.'

He stared at me, his face a frozen mask of undisguised horror.

'I do not understand. What has happened that means we can no longer be together?'

'I will tell you by and by, my lord. But

163

first, I must tell you the whole story, from the beginning.

'When you first beheld me in the forest, I was accompanied by two others — my sisters. We were born at the same time, and we spent the first sixteen years of our lives with our mother on the Lost Island.'

'The Lost Island?' my lord asked. 'What is that?'

'It is an island that is located in a distant ocean, and it is so named because it can only be discovered by chance. Even those who have visited it in the past may never find it again. During those first sixteen years, we knew nothing of our father, save one thing.'

'What was that?'

'Each morning our mother would take us to a high mountain, from whence we could look across the seas towards a distant land. That land, she told us, was the kingdom of Albany. It was the place of our birth, and it should be our rightful home. Indeed, she said, the land would have been our home, had it not been for our father's wrongdoing. But as to the particular nature of that wrongdoing, she kept a firm silence.

'Then, on our seventeenth birthday, we ventured to ask our mother to tell us of the sin which our father had committed, and which had thus exiled us from the land of our birth. She was reluctant at first to divulge it, but then, on accepting that we were now on the verge of adulthood, and thus of an age where we might fully comprehend the tale, she told us the whole story.

'We knew that our mother possessed some form of magical powers, but we did not until then understand that she was a most powerful fae princess. Her name was Pressina. Our father, she told us, was Elinas, the King of Albany. His first wife had died whilst giving birth to their first child, a boy, whom they named Nathas. Elinas was grief-stricken for many years, until such time as he had been persuaded by his courtiers to divert himself by a day's hunting.

'Accordingly, he set out into the forest and became absorbed in hunting a white stag. The stag eluded him, but in the heat of the chase he became very thirsty, and was most relieved when he heard the sound of running water. Following the sound in search of a means of quenching his thirst, he became aware that it was not merely the sound of water but also the sound of singing. Upon entering a clearing, he discovered a fountain of pure sparkling water, by the side of which he beheld my mother. He was captivated by her beauty, and asked her, there and then, to be his wife.'

'Thus it was when I first beheld you,' my lord murmured.

'Indeed so,' I replied. 'And, as it was with us, so it was with my parents. My mother agreed to be the king's wife, subject to one condition: that if she were to bear him any children, he must promise not to visit her at the time of their birth. He readily agreed to this condition, and gave her his solemn promise that he would abide by her wishes. They were married less than a month later.'

'Were they happy?' my lord asked.

'They were, although sadly their happiness was destined to be short-lived. Within a year, my mother gave birth to three daughters: myself, and my sisters Melior and Palatina, all born at a single confinement. Her stepson Nathas hastened to tell his father — our father — the good news. Our father, overjoyed, forgot his promise, and hastened to our mother's chamber . . .'

I felt my dear lord's hand tighten over my own. The parallels between our story and that of my parents were becoming ever more striking.

'What happened?' he asked, in a hoarse whisper.

'He burst through the door of our mother's chamber as she was in the process of bathing us. She turned at the sound, and on seeing him standing there, she cried out 'Alas, my lord, you have broken your word — and hence, alas, we must leave you.' So saying, she gathered myself and my sisters into her arms, and by means of her magical powers she caused us all to disappear, then and there, from our father's sight.'

'And it was from thence that you went to the Lost Island?' my lord asked.

'It was. And it was there that we spent the next sixteen years.'

'What happened next?'

'Once I and my sisters had learned the truth of what our father had done, we were

167

angry and upset by turns. In the fullness of time, my own anger grew so fierce that I devised a plan for revenge upon him. I informed my sisters of the plan, and they too agreed to help me carry it to execution.'

My lord's countenance now bore an expression of undisguised shock and horror.

'I find it impossible to believe, my lady, that you should be capable of planning revenge upon anyone,' he murmured.

'I was young and foolish, my lord. And such folly has, alas, proved to be my own undoing.'

'How so? What folly was that?'

'I and my sisters set out in secret from the Lost Island and made our way across the sea to the kingdom of Albany. There, we made our way to the court of King Elinas, where we presented ourselves as princesses from a foreign land. The king had not set eyes on us since the day of our birth, and he had no notion that we were the same three daughters who had vanished from his life, along with their mother, so many years earlier. He and his courtiers made us most welcome, and prepared quarters for us within the palace.

'Here we remained for three days and three nights. On the morn of the fourth day, we proposed to the king that we should explore a little of the lands around the castle. He readily agreed to conduct us on a tour of those lands. Accordingly, we set out from the castle and set course for the mountain of Brandelois. Upon arriving there, I cast a charm which caused a great chasm to appear in the side of the mountain. Our father dismounted from his horse and stepped inside — whereupon I cast another charm which closed the chasm upon him, trapping him inside.'

I paused in my tale, for now I was weeping freely. Although I had for many years had occasion to rue the folly of my actions, it was only now, as I was relating them to my dearest lord, that I absorbed the full import of what I had done.

He surrounded me with his arms and drew me close to him.

'And do you regret what you did, my lady?'

'I will regret my actions for the rest of my days, my lord. And not merely because of what I did to my father, but also because of what my stupidity has brought upon myself.'

'I do not understand. What you have told me has surprised and shocked me, but I am nonetheless prepared to forgive you for what you did. I fail to comprehend why it should come between us.'

I drew a deep breath before replying.

'I am sorry, my lord, but there is yet more to this sorry tale. When we returned to the Lost Island (for, like our mother, we possessed the power to succeed in finding it whilst others might fail), we told our mother what we had done. But, far from being pleased that we had finally brought such revenge on our father for his having wronged her, she became angry beyond all measure, and vowed to take revenge on us for what she called our 'unnatural action'. She condemned my sisters to wander the earth for seven years, during which time if they ever encountered any human — man, woman or child — they would vanish and never be seen again.'

'So — those companions who were with

170

you by the fountain ... ?'

I nodded sadly. 'Ay, my lord, they were my sisters.'

'And ...' He hesitated, as if summoning up the courage to continue. 'And ... That night — did it fall within the seven years?'

'It was the very last night of the seven years, my lord. We were all four-and-twenty.'

'So that was why they disappeared?'

I nodded again. 'But please, my lord, do not blame yourself for this. You had no notion of what would happen by your chancing upon us that night. The blame for this is mine and mine alone. And now I must suffer my own punishment.'

'What punishment is that? And why did you not vanish as your sisters did?'

'Our mother, perceiving that it had been I who had first conceived the plan of revenge against our father, devised that my punishment should be far more severe than that of my sisters. They, after all, could arrange their lives so that they could remain out of contact with humans. But as for me, our mother laid a vengeful curse upon me: that for one day in every seven, on the day before the holy Sabbath, my lower quarters should shrivel up and become a scaly tail, such as one would see on a fish or a serpent. This curse would remain until such time as I should meet a man who would accept me and marry me, on condition that he should promise never to see me on a Saturday, and that he should keep his word.'

My lord was silent. When he spoke again, his voice was heavy with grief.

'I broke my word to you, just as your father broke his word to your mother. What punishment do you have in store for me?'

'For my part, I would fain have no punishment whatsoever fall upon you. If the choice were mine, I should forgive you, and hope that we could turn our backs upon this dire misadventure and continue with our lives together. And indeed, I do forgive you, with all my heart, but alas, the outcome of this sad event is preordained, and is not within my power to counteract.'

'What, then, will happen?' he whispered. 'What will become of us?'

'Alas, my lord, I must now leave you. For ever. You will live out the remainder of your life until such time as it should naturally run its course, but I am now pledged to wander the earth, condemned to a lonely immortality . . .'

'No!' he shouted. 'Please tell me this is not true!'

I shook my head sadly. 'I am sorry, my lord. I have deceived you for far too long. I would that what I have told you now is untrue, but alas . . .'

'I have brought this upon myself!' he sobbed. 'I could not keep my word to you, and my punishment is that I must now lose you!' His last words were lost in a near-bestial howl.

'One more word, I beg you, my dear lord, before I must depart. Please believe me when I tell you that I bear you no grudge, nor wish you any harm, for what you have done. All I ask of you is that you take good care of our sons, and tell them that their mother will always love them. And please believe me too when I tell you that I have always loved you, and will continue to love you for ever.'

He held out his arms for a last embrace. I touched his lips with my own, then turned *away from him as my form melted into a shapeless mist and drifted out through the open casement . . .*

17

Saturday

'Ray, I told you that I was studying medieval French history and folklore. That was true up to a point, but what I couldn't tell you is that I am actually part of that history and folklore. Have you ever heard the story of Melusine?'

'No, I can't say I have. What happened to her?'

'Not to her, Ray. To me. And it's still happening now. And once I've told you the whole story, I will have to leave you, just like I had to leave my husband, and find somewhere else to spend the rest of eternity.'

She saw him open his mouth as if to speak, but no words came out. He was still staring, transfixed, at her mermaid's tail. Realising that he was not going to answer, she took another sip of water and carried on.

'I was born hundreds of years ago. My

mother was a fae princess who married an ordinary mortal. I had two sisters, born at the same time, and we were brought up by our mother. When we were children we knew nothing about our father, except that he was a king, and our mother hinted that he'd done something very bad. When we turned seventeen she finally told us that just after we were born he'd broken a promise he'd previously made to her, and because of that she'd had to leave him. So my sisters and I decided to take revenge on him for it.' She paused, and shuddered. 'I'd rather not talk about what we did. We thought our mother would be pleased that we'd righted the wrong he'd done her, but when we told her what we'd done, she was furious with us. She — what is the phrase you have? — went ballistic. As I said, she was a fae — I think you call it a faerie — and she used her powers to put a curse on us all. My sisters' punishment was to spend seven years in complete isolation, but because I was the one who had devised and carried out the plan, her revenge on me was much worse. She decreed that I would live for ever, but that I would never find love and happiness with any man on earth.'

'A curse, you say?' Ray finally found his voice.

'Yes. This curse.' Mel gestured towards her tail, which was glistening with a strange silvery-blue lustre. 'We were all banished from the castle, and for the rest of eternity, I would be transformed, every Saturday, into this dreadful half-human, half-fish creature that you're seeing now.'

'So — how did you meet your husband?'

'After our mother cast us out, we went to live in the forest. Like her, we also had magical powers, so we made ourselves a small house, well hidden by the trees, where we could live in secret, and also where I could hide myself away every Saturday when I was transformed. We lived there for seven years. Then, one night, we heard a strange noise in the forest, close to our home. It sounded like a man weeping.'

'And was it?'

Mel nodded. 'His name was Raimondin. When he saw us, my sisters vanished — for reasons which I won't go into here — but I stayed. He told me that he'd been out hunting with his master, the Count of Poitou, but that they'd become separated from the rest of the party and had got lost in the forest. When it went dark they'd set up camp, but they were attacked by a wild boar. Raimondin had tried to fight it, but in the dark he'd accidentally stabbed his master and killed him. I helped him to create a story which would mean he wouldn't end up getting the blame for it.'

Ray stared at her. There was a strange expression in his eyes — one which Mel had never seen before. It frightened her.

He clearly doesn't believe a word of this, she thought. But it's too late now — I'll have to carry on. What difference will it make, anyway, now that he knows? It's all over.

'Raimondin asked me to marry him, and I agreed, but on one condition:

178

that I must spend every Saturday on my own, and that nobody — including him — must ever intrude on my privacy. He agreed, and we were married soon afterwards. I used my powers to build him a castle at Vouvant. I also built one for each of our sons.'

'What? You had children?'

'Yes, several. All boys.' She gave a wry smile. 'I have no need to fear the effects of those fertility dolls. It's a bit late for that! Anyway, one of our sons became a monk, and the others all became soldiers. But they had all been born disfigured in some way, and then rumours started to circulate about me —'

'What sort of rumours?'

'People were wondering why I didn't appear to be looking any older, why all our children were disfigured, and why I locked myself away every Saturday. Raimondin, against his better judgement, was persuaded to find out. So he secretly spied on me, and one Saturday he saw me in mermaid form. He said nothing about it for months, until one day when we had some dreadful news. One of our sons had attacked and burned the abbey where his brother was a monk. Raimondin lost his temper and called me a vile creature who had contaminated his noble race. He apologised as soon as he'd said it, but then admitted that he'd broken his promise to leave me alone every Saturday. At that point, I knew that my cover was blown and I'd have to leave him.'

Ray stared at her. 'These powers that you mentioned — do you still have them?'

'Yes, but only up to the point where I need them for my own survival. For instance, I can speak enough to get by in any language I need, and I can pick up any skill without needing to be taught. I always have the right paperwork. I never run out of money, wherever I am or whatever I'm doing.' She sighed. 'And I never age. I've been twenty-four for hundreds of years.'

Ray gasped. 'Hundreds of years? So what happened to you in the meantime?'

'I travelled. It was always the same,

though, wherever I went. If I met someone special, I had to go on lying and pretending, just like I've had to do with you. They soon grew tired of it, and I had to move on. But I've caused all sorts of mermaid stories along the way. There was a pretty famous one in Denmark. You might have heard about that one — there's even a statue in Copenhagen. But there have been lots of others too. There was the story in France, of course, but also one in Cornwall, one in the Scottish islands — I'm even supposed to be buried on the beach there . . .' She gave a sheepish smile. 'And that story you told me about Columbus . . . Well, you can draw your own conclusion about that.'

Ray was staring at her as if seeing her for the very first time. 'What about this thesis you said you're writing? Is that a lie too?'

Mel sighed. 'No. I am writing something, but it's just a memoir. I needed a plausible excuse for being here, and that seemed as good a reason as any. It's on the computer on my desk. You can read it if you like, after I've gone. It will fill in all the details I've missed.'

Ray glanced across towards the door which led through to Mel's bed-sitting room, but didn't move. 'So . . . All that history that you knew . . . ?'

'Yes. I knew it because I was living at the time when it all happened.'

Ray whistled under his breath. 'That's absolutely mindblowing.'

'Yes,' Mel murmured. 'I suppose it is . . . But now you know everything about me, except one thing. I know I'll never see you again, but I can't leave you without telling you that I love you — more than you can possibly imagine. These past few days with you have made me happier than I have ever been in my entire life, and it breaks my heart to think that we can never be together.'

For a long moment Ray said nothing, then he eased himself to his feet and walked over to the bathtub. He knelt down on the floor, took hold of Mel's hand, and with his other hand reached up and smoothed her hair away from her forehead.

'What makes you think we can never be together?' he murmured.

Mel blinked away a tear. 'Well, now that you've seen me like this . . .'

'It doesn't matter. Yes, I know it's incredible, but once I've got used to the idea, I can live with it. Even if you do need to shut yourself away every Saturday, we'll still have six days out of seven. I'd rather put up with not seeing you for one day a week than not seeing you ever again.'

'Even though I'm a freak?'

'You aren't a freak, my darling. You're just a very, very special person. You're you. And I love you for being just you. Promise me that whatever happens, you will never leave me.'

His hand had found its way into her hair and he gently drew her face towards his own. As their mouths joined, his arms tightened around her and she melted into his warm embrace. At last, she thought, *I have truly come home*.

'I promise,' she whispered, as they

finally drew apart.

He pulled back just far enough to look at her face, and there was no mistaking the message in those wonderful dark eyes.

Then he glanced down, and gasped. His jaw dropped.

'Ray — what's wrong?'

'Your tail. It's gone.'

Mel followed his gaze. Where, moments before, her tail had been, there were now legs. She hastily grabbed a towel and thrust it across her lap to cover her confusion.

'I don't understand,' she whispered. 'You've seen me as a mermaid, yet you're still here. And so am I.'

And then it struck her.

'Ray — I think you might have broken the curse. You've accepted me for what I am. That was the one thing which Raimondin couldn't do. That was why I had to leave him, and why I've stayed like this for so long.'

'Does this mean you'll stop turning into a mermaid?'

Mel's face broke into a slow smile. 'I don't know. Ask me again next Saturday.'

Epilogue

The picturesque fortified village of Vouvant nestles prettily on the edge of the Mervent forest, between the south Vendée towns of La Chataigneraie and Fontenay-le-Comte. Its skyline of pale stone buildings topped with terracotta pantiled roofs is presided over majestically by the magnificent Norman church, visible for miles around.

Arriving in the Place de l'Église, Ray parked the car outside the *mairie* and the two of them stepped out into the warm sunshine. Shielding his eyes from the bright light, he gazed up at the intricate carvings which adorned the west front of the church on the opposite side of the square.

'That's an amazing building. Has the place changed much from what you remember?'

Mel glanced around. 'The church is the same, but the *mairie* is more recent. And I think there are a few more tourists

186

than there used to be.'

'Like that lot over there, you mean?'

He pointed towards a group of people heading towards them, led by a well-dressed, bespectacled man holding up a flag. As they drew nearer, Mel and Ray could hear that the leader, who they guessed must be in his mid to late sixties, was addressing the group in perfect English.

'. . . originally built in the eleventh century,' he was saying, 'by the monks of Maillezais Abbey, under the instructions of William, Duke of Aquitaine. But they ran out of money and could only manage to put up a temporary chapel. The Norman-style building you see today was extensively rebuilt in the twelfth century.'

'This sounds fascinating,' Ray whispered to Mel. 'Do you mind if we join you?' he asked the tour guide, as they attached themselves to the edge of the group.

'Not at all. Welcome!'

'How much do we owe you?'

'Nothing! This is my pleasure.' The guide beamed at them, then went on to describe how the church had undergone another restoration in the late nineteenth century, which had resulted in the church's unusual octagonal tower.

'The original plan was for this to have a spire on top,' he explained, 'but for some reason this was never built, and the tower was finished with the tiled roof that you can see today.'

'They probably ran out of money, too,' muttered someone in the group. Mel caught Ray's eye, nodded and winked.

The guide laughed. 'Maybe. But whatever the reason, I must admit I'm rather glad. I can't imagine it with a spire. I think it looks much more impressive like this.'

'But why build here?' asked another member of the group. 'It seems a rather odd choice of place.'

'It might seem like that to us nowadays,' the guide answered, 'but back in the Middle Ages things looked rather different. France was divided into a number of separate, self-governing territories, and where we are now is the northern limit of the Duchy of Aquitaine. Duke William wanted to protect the frontier, and he chose to build a fortified settlement here because it's easy to defend. The village is built on a rock which is surrounded by the river on three sides. It would be virtually impossible to attack. And now, if you'd all care to follow me, we will take a look at the ramparts and the *Tour Melusine*.'

Ray glanced at his watch. 'Shall we do that?' he whispered to Mel. 'We've got a bit of time before we —'

Mel squeezed his hand and grinned. 'Yes, let's,' she whispered back. 'I'd love to hear what he has to say . . .'

They followed the guide along the narrow streets to an open grassy area fringed by trees. He led them across to the far side, where a thick, waist-high grey wall commanded a magnificent view of the river and the surrounding forest.

'This,' he told them, 'is the River Mère.'

'*Mer*' as in 'sea'?' one of the group asked.

'No, '*mère*' as in 'mother'. It's a rather clever play on words, but the local people regard the river as the mother of the village. And, as I mentioned earlier, it protects the place from invaders. This is why the castle was built here, where we're standing now. Originally, the castle occupied the whole of this area, but much of it was demolished in the nineteenth century. All that remains of it now are these ramparts and the old keep. It was built in the Middle Ages by the Lusignan family, but according to legend, the castle was built in one night by the faerie Melusine.'

'Faerie?' Ray asked, sounding puzzled. 'I've heard something about this legend, but I'd always understood that Melusine was a mermaid.'

'Well, yes, up to a point,' the guide answered. 'She had a mermaid's tail — or some say it was a serpent's tail. But she had faerie blood in her. Her mother was a faerie, but her father was human. Anyway, the story goes that she built this castle in a single night, with just an apronful of stones and a mouthful of water.'

A gasp went round the group.

'And not just this castle,' the guide went on, 'but also six others on the surrounding hills. One of those, at Tiffauges, is believed to be the original Bluebeard's castle.'

'You seem to know a lot about local history,' Mel remarked.

The guide beamed. 'It's my job — and my passion. I used to be a history teacher before I retired and moved here. The story of Melusine has always been one of my favourites. Some believe that she returns from time to time, keeping watch over the village. And now, let's go and look at the tower . . .'

'Thank you,' Ray answered, glancing again at his watch. 'It's been fascinating hearing about this. But will you please excuse us? We're supposed to be somewhere else in twenty minutes.'

'Of course. *Bonne journée!*'

'You never mentioned Bluebeard,' Ray

murmured to Mel, as the group moved off.

'That's because he wasn't my son. Thank goodness!' She shuddered. 'But it just shows how stories can become distorted over time.'

Ray nodded. 'What was it the guide said? '*She returns from time to time...*' I must confess I feel rather sorry for him. He had no idea how close he was! But come on. We need to make our way back. We mustn't be late for our appointment with *Monsieur le Maire*. I just hope my French is up to the task.'

* * *

The mayor of Vouvant smiled at them across his desk, as the two members of the town hall staff who were acting as witnesses stood respectfully alongside him. He cleared his throat and addressed Ray and Mel formally in turn with the words of the French marriage ceremony.

'Raymond David Wynn Jones, voulez-vous prendre comme légitime épouse Melusine

192

Clémence de Lusignan, ici présente?'

If the mayor had noticed the significance of the bride's name, he was tactful enough not to remark on it. Or maybe, Mel thought as she remembered how she herself had struggled with the 'w' sound, he was just concentrating on trying to pronounce Ray's name correctly. Ray glanced at Mel as he gripped her hand, then turned back to the mayor and proudly answered, *'Oui.'*

'Melusine Clémence de Lusignan, voulez-vous prendre comme légitime époux Raymond David Wynn Jones, ici présent?'

I still can't quite believe this is happening, Mel thought. But aloud she said a simple, grateful *'Oui.'*

* * *

The two of them stood leaning against the safety railings on the top of the Tour Melusine, pausing in the warm light breeze to catch their breath after climbing the vast spiral staircase. Above them, mounted on a pole on the top of a small turret, was a simple two-dimensional figure in the form of a mermaid with a long, curled, serpent-like tail: Melusine keeping watch over her castle and her lands.

Mel stared out across the village, the countryside and the forest. 'It feels strange to be standing up here again, after all this time. And on a Saturday, too.' She glanced down at her feet. 'But I shouldn't have tried climbing all those stairs in these fancy shoes.'

'I though you said you weren't a shoe person.'

'I'm not. There didn't seem to be much point in getting excited about footwear when I didn't always have feet. But today is a special occasion. Worth making a bit of effort, I think!'

'So what are you, exactly? Mermaid? Faerie? Serpent?'

'No, none of those. Well, not any more. I'm just an ordinary person. At long last.'

'Any regrets?'

Mel shook her head. 'None at all. I'm just so glad it's all over.' She brushed away a tear and turned to face him. 'Thank you for marrying me. But are you sure I'm not too old for you?'

'Mrs Jones, you don't look a day over twenty-five.'

Mel grinned. "Mrs Jones'? I think I like the sound of my new name. But seriously, *chéri*, I want to grow old with you. I've had quite enough of eternal youth and immortality. They're definitely overrated.'

Ray smiled. 'Did you notice that café that we passed on the way here?'

'Which one?'

'The *Café Melusine*. Do you fancy a coffee?'

Mel reached out and took his hand. 'A proper coffee? That would be wonderful . . .'

Author's Afterword

Mel — Folklore or Fact

Sometimes a whole story can be triggered off by just one sudden flash of inspiration. In the case of *Never on Saturday*, this was a single line of dialogue: *My name isn't Melanie — it's Melusine*.

The tale of Melusine is a traditional French legend. It forms the basis of *Never on Saturday*, although I've taken one or two liberties with the ending. In some versions of the original story Melusine is depicted as half-woman, half-serpent, and this is how she appears at the top of the *Tour Melusine* in Vouvant, Western France.

In other images she has two tails — and in fact this is the source of the modern-day *Starbucks* logo. But for the purposes of this story, I preferred to portray her as a conventional-looking mermaid: a beautiful woman, but with a fish tail instead of legs.

Mermaids and mermen have been part of folklore for thousands of years, though opinions vary about their probable origins. One suggestion is that the first known example was a fish-tailed god called Oannes, who was worshipped as Lord of the Seas in ancient Babylon. Another source could have been a Syrian legend dating from around 1,000 BCE. The goddess Atargatis dived into a lake to take the form of a fish, but she was not allowed to give up her great beauty — so only her bottom half became a fish, whilst above the waist she kept her human form. Greek and Roman mythology contains lots of water sprites, many of whom had fish tails. The mermaid was one of the symbols of Aphrodite, the Greek goddess of love and beauty. Homer's epic poem The Odyssey includes an episode in which 'The Sirens' sang to attract sailors to their doom, and some mythologists believe that these 'Sirens' would have been in mermaid form. Indeed, the French word for mermaid is *la sirène*.

Some of the legends of the Pacific Islands suggest that human beings are descended from both mermaids and mermen. It seems that somewhere back in time their tails somehow dropped off, and people were magically able to walk on land. A good example of this is the creator god Vatea, who was usually depicted as being half-human and half-fish.

It was once believed that aquamarine (called the gemstone of the sea) came from the tears of mermaids, and had the power to protect sailors when they were at sea.

Towards the end of the Middle Ages, when maritime trade began to expand, mermaids became central to sailor folk-lore. For sailors (who were almost always men), mermaids came to represent the wonder, mystery and danger of a life at sea. Mermaid images could be found on inn signs, heraldic crests, tattoos, scrimshaw, and the bows of ships. Mermaid lore owes much to the various stories of water nymphs from different lands, including the shape-shifting *rusalki* of Slavic mythology, and the selkies of Scottish, Irish, Scandinavian and Icelandic folklore. The latter were creatures which lived as seals in the sea but changed to human form on dry land.

Many places claim their own individual mermaid legends. A few of these are referred to in Chapter Seventeen of *Never on Saturday*.

The island of Benbecula, in the Outer Hebrides, is believed to be the last resting place of a mermaid who was washed up on the beach at Culla Bay in 1830. One account at the time stated:

'The upper part of the creature was about the size of a well-fed child of three or four years of age, with abnormally developed breasts. The hair was long, dark and glossy, while the skin was white, soft and tender. The lower part of the body was like a salmon, but without scales.'

The description suggests that this particular 'mermaid' might have been a child who suffered from a very rare medical condition called Sirenomelia, in which the legs are fused together so that they resemble a mermaid's tail.

St Senara's church at Zennor in Cornwall contains a decorated carved wooden seat called the Mermaid Chair. According to legend, a mermaid is said to have fallen in love with the church's chief chorister, a youth named Matthew Trewhella, and charmed him away to her home under the sea.

In addition, there are many recorded 'sightings' of mermaids at sea, including one by Christopher Columbus in 1493. He described them as *not half as beautiful as they are painted*. In fact, as Ray explains to Mel, they were not mermaids at all, but manatees: slow-moving aquatic mammals with seal-like tails, bulbous faces and human-looking eyes.

The practice of producing fake mummified mermaids (such as the one featured in The Palace of Curiosities in the story) probably dates back to the 19th Century. They usually consisted of the tail of a fish attached either to the top half of a monkey, or to a human-like head, arms and torso made from papier-mâché built on a wire frame. Sometimes real teeth were added for extra effect. The fake mermaids came originally from the Far East and Asia, and were made by fishermen who sold them to supplement their income. One famous example was the Feejee Mermaid, first exhibited by P T Barnum at his museum in New York in 1843. Although the publicity for the mermaid implied that she was a beautiful living creature, the reality could hardly have been more different. Barnum himself later went on to say in his autobiography that the mermaid was *an ugly, dried-up, black-looking, and diminutive specimen . . . its arms thrown up, giving it the appearance of having died in great agony*. In addition to the particularly fine example on display at The Palace of Curiosities, other fake mermaids can still be seen in museums today, including the Buxton Museum in Derbyshire and the Horniman Museum in south London.

In modern mythology, mermaids

are more likely to be seen as innocent, sweet, helpful and self-sacrificing. Much of this interpretation can probably be credited to the most famous mermaid tale of all — Hans Christian Andersen's *The Little Mermaid*.

MELUSINE

It is believed that Melusine's name is derived from *Mère des Lusignan* (the Mother of the Lusignans).

The first known version of the Melusine story dates from the late 14th Century, and was chronicled by Jean D'Arras, secretary to the Duc de Berry. According to D'Arras, Melusine (or Melusina) was one of the three daughters of Helmas (King of Scotland) and his wife, a water-fae named Pressina. Helmas had fallen in love with Pressina after finding her singing beside a fountain. She agreed to marry him on condition that if she should bear him any children, he should never visit her until she had risen from her bed after the birth. In due course she gave birth to triplet daughters (Melior, Plantina and Melusina), but on hearing the news of the birth Helmas forgot his promise and rushed to Pressina's bedside. Pressina was devastated at what she saw as a betrayal of Helmas's word, and took up her three baby daughters in her arms and vanished. She brought up her daughters alone until they were fifteen, when she told them the truth about their father.

Melusina was determined to take revenge on Helmas for what he had done to their mother, and contrived with her sisters to trap him and imprison him in the heart of a mountain. But when Pressina found out what Melusina had done she was furious, and sentenced her daughter to lonely immortality, forced to spend every Saturday in mermaid form.

Melusine subsequently married Raimondin de Poitou. As described in *Never on Saturday*, they lived happily together for many years, during which time Melusine spent every Saturday in total seclusion, but she was forced to leave Raimondin when he eventually discovered her secret. According to legend, Melusine still keeps watch over the lands around Vouvant. If she is seen, this foretells the death of a king.

Jean D'Arras's work was later developed by Stephan, a Dominican of the House of Lusignan. He made the story so famous that various noble families, including the House of Luxembourg, altered their pedigrees to make it appear that they were descended from Melusine. Indeed, King Richard I of England is reported to have made the same claim.

This, however, may have been a mixed blessing. Elizabeth Woodville (who became the wife of King Edward IV of England and subsequently the mother of the Princes in the Tower) was the daughter of Jacquetta of Luxembourg, who was the 5x-great-granddaughter of King Henry III of England. Despite this illustrious ancestry, Elizabeth was still regarded as a commoner — and as a result her marriage to King Edward was, to say the least, controversial. Her enemies could not countenance the idea of the King marrying for love, rather than making a marriage of alliance with a foreign princess. They began to spread rumours that Elizabeth had used witchcraft to seduce him, and that her mother Jacquetta had used magic to bewitch him into marrying her daughter.

So how did this fictional story come to be regarded as fact? One possible explanation is that Melusine of Lusignan is sometimes confused with the real-life Melisende, who was Queen of Jerusalem in the early 12th Century. The confusion may have arisen because of the similarity of the two names, but, intriguingly, there is a tenuous link between the two stories. The crown of Jerusalem, which was passed through the female line, was subsequently inherited by Melisende's granddaughter Sybilla — who then passed it to her husband: Guy de Lusignan.

Melisende's husband was Fulk V,

Count of Anjou. He was a wealthy and prominent crusader, and latterly a strong supporter of the Knights Templar.

Could the real-life Melisende of Jerusalem have in fact been Jewish (either by origin or by conversion), but afraid to admit her faith to her Christian husband or to any members of his court? If so, could this be one source of the story that she had to hide herself away every Saturday — to secretly observe the Jewish sabbath? One can only speculate . . .

Sue Barnard
December 2020

We do hope that you have enjoyed reading this large print book.

Did you know that all of our titles are available for purchase?

We publish a wide range of high quality large print books including:
Romances, Mysteries, Classics
General Fiction
Non Fiction and Westerns

Special interest titles available in large print are:
The Little Oxford Dictionary
Music Book, Song Book
Hymn Book, Service Book

Also available from us courtesy of Oxford University Press:
Young Readers' Dictionary
(large print edition)
Young Readers' Thesaurus
(large print edition)

For further information or a free brochure, please contact us at:
Ulverscroft Large Print Books Ltd.,
The Green, Bradgate Road, Anstey,
Leicester, LE7 7FU, England.
Tel: (00 44) **0116 236 4325**
Fax: (00 44) **0116 234 0205**

THE GENTLEMAN GYPSY

Sarah Swatridge

1900. Ruth is in need of an income; meanwhile, handsome but eccentric Newham needs someone to care for his animals while he roams the country in his horse-drawn caravan. Ruth, too, is unconventional, and can often be seen cycling around the village helping those less fortunate than herself. The two set off to explore the land together — and their friendship may even turn into something more . . .

A GIFT OF A DUKE

Fenella J. Miller

Miss Mirabelle Thompson, having believed herself a penniless orphan, is astonished to discover that she is an heiress. Immediately she rents a house in Cavendish Square and commences her new life. Meanwhile, the new Duke of Clonmel is equally astonished to discover, upon inheriting the title from his brother, that the estate is forfeit and all he has are debts. He has only one way out of this sticky situation — and that is to seek a rich bride in London . . .

AN IMPERFECT CHRISTMAS

Tanya Jean Russell

Maggie Green thought she had her life perfectly on track: a long-term relationship, a successful career in finance, and a swanky apartment in London. But then everything falls apart. She's made redundant, dumped by her boyfriend, and there's a worrying call from her doctor. With her pride in tatters, Maggie returns to her family home for the Christmas period. No one knows the real reason she hasn't been back — except the one person she is most nervous about seeing again . . .